QuizQuester
and the
Captive Of The Illusionist

This summer hang out with your friends and read your book from MECU.
Municipal Employees Credit Union of Baltimore, Inc.

This summer hang out with your friends and read your book from MECU.
Municipal Employees Credit Union of Baltimore, Inc.

This summer hang out with your friends and read your book from MECU.
Municipal Employees Credit Union of Baltimore, Inc.

Captive of The Illusionist

Bert and Tim Brocato

Editor
Mary Brocato

Cover Art
Gail Cross

Inside Illustrations
Jared Barlow, Jessie Brocato, and J.D. Parnell

Library of Congress Catalog Card Number: **2002092121**

ISBN **0-9718432-0-1**

Published by QuizQuester Press, LLC
127 Edgewood Ave., Baltimore, MD 21228

Printed in the United States of America

An Exciting Learn By Choice Adventure Book

QuizQuester
AND THE
Captive Of The Illusionist

Bert and Tim Brocato

Q Q
QuizQuester Press
Baltimore, Maryland

Book One of Six
in the
QuizQuester seventh grade series

COMING WINTER 2002
Book Two
QuizQuester
and the
Lost Treasure

CONTENTS

Note to Reader

If this is your first Learn By Choice adventure, this book is unlike any you have ever read before. It is designed to read like a regular novel and yet give you the fun of choosing your own path. This book will be fun for anyone who likes a challenging puzzle or just a great story.

It is important to note that when you come to choices there will be four different choices. You need to remember the page you are on when you choose your answer.

Example:
You are on page 29.
While on page 29, you choose answer 'C', which says turn to page 52.
When you turn to page 52, you need to remember that you came from page 29.
On page 52, you will find "From page 29", and you will be directed where to go from there.
It's easy after you do your first one.

About Our Web Site

Come visit us at quizquester.com. On our web site, you will be able to take FREE pretests for the standardized achievement tests. Plus, you will see what books we currently have available and hear updates about our progress.

Chapter One
Home Safely

"What sentence do you pronounce on the accused?"

"Guilty! Deep freeze and send him off into deep space!" you yell.

"Very well," replies the Space Master. "Max Rainer, you have been found guilty of conspiracy and sedition against the Martian Colony. Your sentence is to be sent off into deep space where you will age two years and during which the time on Mars will pass 40 years without your influence."

On your monitor, you watch as the door to the cryo-chamber closes over Max, and the chamber fills with a cloudy vapor. A member of the High Guard sets the clock above the chamber. After a few seconds, the scene on the monitor changes showing you Max's ship leaving space dock and blasting off into space.

"We hope you have enjoyed playing *Crimson Planet*, another role game by GameLenz." You have finally finished the game. It has taken you all week.

"Carter, off," you say to your computer.

Back in the real world, your thoughts of your game mix with that of your surroundings. You are waiting with your sister, Deborah, on a bench on the school's front porch. The school building has always reminded you of an antiquated, two-story mansion. Stately pillars stand on the covered-porch. The siding consists of tan stucco. White, replica-wood shutters frame the windows, and the roof is covered with stone gray, synthetic-slate tiles.

You daydream about playing an adventure in older times, an adventure in which you live in a mansion.

2

Your thoughts are interrupted when you see your mom. You know it is Mom because you see the mini-FTV with four wheels. Most kids at your school are affluent enough to afford the newer model, family, hover vehicles. In spite of that, you silently thank God that your parents are well off enough to send you to New Haven Academy.

A mass of kids are milling around in the well-manicured courtyard, so your mom doesn't see you. The picture before you of the kids in their school uniforms reminds you of penguins. A plaid, green-and-navy-blue jumper with white blouse adorns the girls. Navy blue pants with a white shirt and blue tie embellishes the boys.

You look at your sister sitting beside you. She is busy doing her homework on her computer and doesn't see your mom pull up. Using her family nickname, you say, "Hey, D.D., Mom's here. Let's go."

D.D. says to her computer, "Vince, put the words, *The Tale of Two Cities*, in italics." She pushes in her adjustable vid-screen and takes out her e-text disk. D.D. looks up from her work. "Let's go then. Where is she?" She puts her computer back into its pouch that she is wearing around her waist. Most kids are wearing similar pouches containing their computers and e-texts. They are almost extensions of their uniforms.

"Over there," you point. "Come on." You and D.D. start to make your way through the courtyard.

On the way, D.D. pauses to talk to one of her teammates on the equestrian team. D.D. is very popular. You don't know how she became so popular in such a short period of time. You don't seem to have half the number of friends even though this is your third year at New Haven.

"D.D., ask your mom again about that equestrian vid-disk. It's totally cool," says D.D.'s friend, Erica.

"I won't forget. Bye."

When you finally reach your mom, she waves to you and says, "We have to hurry. I have an appointment this afternoon."

As you exit through the main gate, you pass by the rolling green fields outside the school. The ninth graders on the equestrian team are riding horses. D.D. wishes she could be there with them, but since she is only in seventh grade, she is not allowed free-ride time yet. She leans toward the car window and puts her head on her folded arms and says in a purposeful, dreamy voice, "Horses are forever."

You can't stand it. D.D. always gets on your nerves by going on about stupid horses. You don't have anything against horses; in fact, you like horses. You just can't stand the way D.D. goes on and on about them.

On the ride home, you ask your mom if you can buy a new *Blak and Wytes* disk from Masc Music since you heard from the kids at school that it was on sale. D.D. pipes in that if you get to buy the music disk, she should be allowed to buy the horse vid-disk that she has wanted.

"Do you have any spare disks with you?" your mom asks.

"No, but I can burn one when I get home. I have plenty of memory to store it until then," you tell her.

"It's on sale, is it? Oh, I guess so. It still seems like a waste of money, but go ahead."

"Cool! Carter, go to Masc Music and download the newest *Blak and Wytes* music collection. Payment is authorized." In a fraction of a second, Carter says in a perfect, upper-class, British voice, "Download complete." You named your computer Carter because you liked the sound of a British accent, and you thought Carter sounded like an appropriate name for a butler.

4

"What about my equestrian vid?" D.D. asks.

"No! That's enough for today."

"But that's not fair. When can I get the equestrian vid?"

"Mom, D.D.'s right; that's not fair," you chime in with your own complaint on your sister's behalf. "It is her own money, isn't it?"

Your mother says nothing in response.

"Well, how about it, Mom?" D.D. asks again.

"Don't ask again. That's enough!"

After a moment's pause, D.D. gives up and mutters something under her breath.

Mom drives to the Mega-Mart. "I ordered some milk and bread on the web earlier. Here's the code." Mom hands the coded disk to you. "Please run up to the window and get it for me."

"Why didn't you have it delivered?" you ask.

"Because I was trying to save some money. I knew we would be driving right by the Mega-Mart."

There is no traffic at the window, so when you put the disk into the slot, the conveyer has your milk and bread waiting for you in two separate sacks. You grab the bags and the disk and are back in the FTV in a flash.

"Next time, can I get the groceries?" D.D. asks.

"Yes, but remind me," Mom says. "When we get home, I have to go out. Your father has an important business meeting tonight, and I am going out for a makeover this afternoon. I want you kids to go straight to your rooms and do your homework before you go outside. And nobody comes in while I'm gone."

You pass by the homes in your neighborhood. You like the Patterson's home because it looks stately. The blue and white house stands handsomely among the trees. Bradford Pears line the wraparound driveway. Though it should have looked normal for your neighborhood as the faux-estate, three-story, colonial variety is typical for the area, it stands out to you. There is something special about the house and property.

D.D. likes the Mick's house. The Mick family has an over-sized, five-acre plot. Most of the other homes have three-acre plots. Theirs is the one with three Arabian horses. The Mick parents let D.D. ride, so she likes their house the best.

When you reach home, your mom pulls into the garage. As you pass by the basketball hoop in the driveway, you think that you might come out later and shoot some hoops.

Your house is different from other houses in the neighborhood. Your home is a geo-house with a southern exposure in the back. It has a southwestern feel to it though the roof is pitched. The house is built into the hill with one story showing in the front and two stories in the back. Its exterior is stucco and brick with a red, clay tile roof. A garage stands to the right on top of the hill. Large, deciduous trees populate the back and sides. There is a small courtyard in the back where two parts of the house extend beyond the main building. On top of the extensions, there are balconies with a hot tub on one and an outdoor grill on the other. Your home is made for low maintenance, comfort, and security.

When the FTV stops, D.D. bounds out, opens your door, and runs to her room downstairs, slamming the door behind her. Both you and your sister have bedrooms downstairs while your parents have their bedroom upstairs with the living room, dining room, and kitchen. You and your mom load the groceries into the fridge-unit and pantry.

"Now don't forget what I told you. I have to go out this afternoon," says your mother. "I want you to get started on your homework right away before you do anything else."

6

You head down to your room and close the door behind you. Your bedroom is located right next to D.D.'s. Your room is painted green with a dark green carpet and matching dark green curtains and bedspread.

You drop your uniform on the messy floor. You decide that today is a good day for fishing rather than basketball, so you change into some military-fatigue pants and don your favorite military boots. You put on a long-sleeved shirt even though it seems a little warm for it. Then, you sit down at your desk to do your homework like you do almost every school day.

Chapter Two
Something's Amiss

Before doing your homework, you burn your *Blak and Wytes* disk from your computer's memory. Still procrastinating, you decide to check your email messages. In the list of messages is one from your sister D.D. You wonder why you would be getting a message from your sister, so you check it first. The message is all in caps. It screams, "HORSES ARE THE BEST!"

You think that D.D. is just trying to get on your nerves again, so you go next door to her room to tell her to knock off the nonsense. As you approach her room, you see smoke coming out from under the closed door.

Pushing open the door, you rush into the room thinking something is wrong. Maybe D.D. is fooling around with candles again, and something has caught on fire. Not far into the room, you trip on something and fall, hitting your head hard on D.D.'s desk chair, which knocks you out cold.

You aren't sure how long you have been out; you don't think it is very long. As you try to sit up, your head is aching, and you feel the room beginning to spin. You have a big knot on your forehead. But, as your head clears and the pain subsides, you see that the smoke in the room is only about two feet high, and there is no apparent source to the swirling mist. There is no apparent D.D. either.

You feel something down by your feet and discover that D.D.'s riding boots caused your fall. You wonder why her chair is so far out into the room. You get up and examine the room more closely. The room seems to be in its usual immaculately clean state except for the boots and the chair. The room is painted blue with a matching dark blue spread, carpet, curtains, and wing-back chair. You check behind the chair but don't see anything. While investigating her closet, you notice her uniform hanging neatly in among the rest of her clothes, but you don't see D.D.

After further examination, you see there are two old-fashioned pieces of paper in the middle of your sister's desk along with her pocket computer. Curious, you pick up the papers. One paper seems to be a note written in script, and the other paper has a map on it that reminds you of a pirate's treasure map.

The note says,

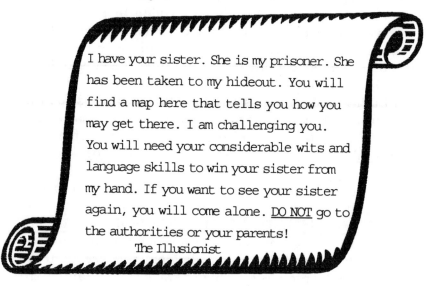

I have your sister. She is my prisoner. She has been taken to my hideout. You will find a map here that tells you how you may get there. I am challenging you. You will need your considerable wits and language skills to win your sister from my hand. If you want to see your sister again, you will come alone. <u>DO NOT</u> go to the authorities or your parents!
The Illusionist

You are shocked. At first, you consider that your sister might be playing some sort of elaborate joke on you: *Can this be real, or is it a joke?* Your nerves are on edge. You can't afford to take a chance on it being a joke. You say to yourself that you must treat it as if it is real even if you don't believe it.

You calm yourself. If this is a real madman that has

your sister, what can you do? Your first inclination is to call your mom on her computer, but then you remember that the note says not to contact your parents.

You think again. Maybe it is a joke. You have one of the best security systems money can buy at your house. It is tied into the police system and everything. You check the window in your sister's room. It is shut and locked. There are no signs of a struggle anywhere. There are no marks on the window. You check the closet again.

You go upstairs to check the security system. It is armed. Your mother must have set it when she went out. Who could have gotten past it? You check every window in the house including the ones upstairs. All are locked, including the doors. The central climate control is on. What if the intruder was already in the house before you got home? You think again. If this is a joke, you have to play along. The stakes are too high–the chance of never seeing D.D. again.

You consider calling the police yourself, but you change your mind. The note says to not go to the authorities. You have to consider your options and do it quickly.

You go to your room to think. You close the door behind you and say a prayer. "Lord, what must I do?" Suddenly, a thought occurs to you.

You get out your pocket computer and say, "Carter, on." The computer blinks on in response. "Carter, my sister has been kidnapped. What should I do?"

"I do not understand the question. Insufficient data to make a query of the database," Carter responds.

"Carter, hook to the net. Look up all the information you can find on a criminal, alias The Illusionist."

"There is no data on a criminal with the name of 'The Illusionist' in the available data."

"Show me any references to the title *The Illusionist.*"

"There are over 2,500 references to the title *The Illusionist* in the available data."

"Carter, are any of them dealing with criminal activity?"

You have to wait a few minutes before the computer responds as it searches through the available data. "There is a fictional book with the title *The Illusionist of Highland Heights* by Max Morgan."

"Carter, are there any plot summaries of the book?"

"Yes, one. The Illusionist is a scientist of considerable skills, but he has a criminal bent."

"Carter, give me all the information you can find on Max Morgan."

"Max Morgan was a pseudo-name for an unknown author. There is an article in the *Miami Herald* historical documents that claim he was a rich philanthropist. The article was written by Steve Stanley, the author of a one-paragraph summary."

"Carter, show me any current information you can find on Steve Stanley. How can I reach him?"

"Steve Stanley is deceased. He died in 2030 and left his inheritance to charity. He has no known relative in the available data."

You think of a few curse words but decide not to use them. "Carter, show me the article by Steve Stanley about the author Max Morgan."

Carter displays the article.

"*The Illusionist of Highland Heights* that hit the net with a splash was a great read. It left you on the edge of your seat wondering what would happen next. Max Morgan, whoever he is, did a fantastic job. The Illusionist seemed like a really twisted criminal with considerable scientific skills. My sources tell me that Max Morgan is actually a very rich philanthropist living in the N.Y.-Philly-D.C. tri-mega-city area, but his name is still unknown."

"Is that it? Carter, find a copy of *The Illusionist of Highland Heights*."

"There are no known copies available for sale or at the libraries."

"Carter, what happened to the book?"

"Unknown. There is a 95% probability that the book has been deleted from all available sources."

You think to yourself that there may be a copy in somebody's private disk collection, but you won't be able to find it.

"Carter, according to the latest police statistics, what is the probability of a kidnapper hurting or killing a victim?"

"There is a 5% probability of a victim being seriously hurt and a 2% probability of death in the U.S. today. Kidnapping is on the decline in the U.S. in recent trends."

That's enough for you. You know you must do something. You get up from your desk and pack your pocket computer into its pouch. You have to go after your sister. Now. You pack all your school disks into your pouch also. You think this is turning out to be like an old-fashioned mystery. Where will it end?

You reread the note from The Illusionist and check the map. After recalling what the note says on needing considerable language skills, you load up the disk on language and grammar into your computer. The map from The Illusionist seems to take you down the highway a bit, but it is sketchy.

You pull your computer back out of its pouch. "Carter, show me a local road map." The vid-screen shows a map of your town.

"Carter, expand the map to include southern

12

Vermont." The map expands. You pull open Carter's vid-screen to its full length and width to look at the map. The two maps coincide on most roads, but the road marked with an "X" on The Illusionist's map is not found on the one that Carter is showing you. There is no road named Mountain Road to be found at the location shown.

"Well, mystery road, it looks like I am going to have to find you."

You decide that you should leave a copy of the note and map at home, but you want to take them with you as well. You go to your father's office to copy the papers.

Your father's office is located downstairs on the other side of the family room directly opposite your bedroom. You walk into the office. You've always liked the way it is decorated. There are shelves with old-fashioned books on them along with plants and various knickknacks. There are replicas of Leonardo da Vinci's paintings on the walls and a few models of his flying machines hanging from the ceiling. There is a big computer that looks like an old-fashioned desktop computer located in the office, along with various accessories like a scanner and copier.

You scan and copy the two papers that you have. You take another piece of paper and scribble an old-fashioned note to your mother.

"Mom, I am going after D.D. to try to get her back. I am sure you will want to go to the police. I have copied the note and the map that I found in her room. Please, don't worry." When you are done, you sign your name and tape the papers to the inside garage door that you know your mom will go through to enter the house. You fold the originals and pack them into your computer pouch along with your computer.

Not wanting to waste anymore time, you put on your leather jacket because you know you will be riding on the highway, and you go out to the garage.

You and your sister, D.D., both have Honda P11 hover bikes in the garage, along with helmets. There are no vehicles in the garage since both parents are out, so your hover bike is easy to get out.

On the way out, you see your basketball along with the fishing equipment amongst the boxes and other junk. You think that basketball and fishing seem like another world to you right now.

Chapter Three
Friendly Neighbor

The note says "do not go to the authorities or your parents," but it doesn't say anything about not going to the neighbor's. You need someone you can trust, and you know just the person.

Mr. Wheatly is a kind old man. He is very nearly one hundred, and you respect the wisdom he has acquired over the years. You ride your hover bike over to his house before heading out on your search.

Mr. Wheatly has been in the neighborhood a long time, and he has an older house. You have helped him do lawn work from time to time in the past. He always paid very well and complimented you on the job you had done.

You ring his bell, and before long, he comes to the door. He moves around very well for someone his age. "Well, hello," he says. "Come in. Come in." He opens the door. You go into his house.

"Mr. Wheatly, I have something very important to talk to you about. I need your advice." There is uncertainty in your voice. You feel a little nervous as you open your pouch and pull out the map and paper. As you hand them to him, you say, "I think something terrible has happened to D.D. I found these in her room."

He quietly takes the note in his hand and begins to read it.

While he is reading it, you say, "I am thinking about going after her. I just wanted your advice before I go. What should I do? What if something really bad has happened to her?"

Mr. Wheatly asks you to tell him, in detail, how you came across the note and the map, so you relate all of the facts to him. You are in a little bit of a frenzy by the time you are done. You are anxious about your sister.

"Whoever The Illusionist is, he is a cunning and crafty man," replies Mr. Wheatly as he peers at you with a concerned look on his face. "He was able to get past your security system without any problem and snatch your sister in a very short time. He left only the evidence that he wanted you to find. I would not underestimate his abilities."

You respond with nervous sarcasm, "You're very comforting."

Wheatly isn't amused. He just keeps the same sober expression on his face. "You have to realize that this is not about your sister. It is about you. Whoever this madman is, he wants you to come to him, and he has gone to a lot of trouble to make it happen."

"Do you think I should go then?"

"I think you have already made up your mind about that, and I won't get in the way. I will only say be brave and courageous and you will have your sister back. I know you are a good student and your language skills are excellent. You should be able to meet his challenge."

"Are you going to call the police yourself?" you ask.

"You know that we should go to the police right away before the trail gets cold. Most of these sorts of things are always solved by going to the police."

"But, Mr. Wheatly, the note says to not go to the authorities. What if he hurts D.D.?"

"I think he has already hurt her, in a way. He has abducted her against her will. Somebody that does that is not to be trusted. Besides, he told *you* not to go to the authorities. He didn't tell me."

"Well, then what should I do?"

"Go after her. We should give this guy a chance to return your sister his way; otherwise, we might not get

16

her back. But we should also go to the police." Wheatly pauses to think. "I will give you a little time before calling the police and trying to reach your parents. I assume you could have called them on their computers?"

"Yes, I just didn't know what to do."

"Don't worry about it then. I will take care of it. You just get going."

"Thank you Mr. Wheatly. If anything happens to me, you should tell my parents that I came here before I left."

"Don't worry. I will. I will be praying for you and your sister. I may know something about The Illusionist. We will see. It may be that you will have more than one chance to rescue your sister."

You don't ask Mr. Wheatly what he means by this last statement because you are in such a hurry. You turn and quickly leave Mr. Wheatly's house and head back out of town on your hover bike. You are frightened, but you are also excited by the challenge, and you know Mr. Wheatly wouldn't let you do anything too dangerous. You know you can handle it. You are also thankful that he is going to call the police. You are thankful to have some professional backup, just in case. Now, it is time to figure out the riddle of your missing sister.

Chapter Four

Hitting The Trail

You aren't really confident about traveling on Highway 91 on your hover bike; it seems quite dangerous to you. Your parents don't let you ride your bike on the highway, and, besides, your P11 isn't highway legal. Your parents wouldn't buy you the bigger Honda P22 since you're not even old enough to have a driver's license. *Oh well*, you think, *I'll deal with it later*.

You look down at the gauge and see that your bike is almost fully charged. Thankfully, the hover bikes run on a lithicad battery and are able to recharge from the sun, so you don't need any fuel.

You speed off down the road as fast as you can safely go. You ride in town with ease for a while until you have the strange sensation that you are being followed. Every time you check the mirror on your handle bar, you think you see something following you, but then it is gone. You stop a couple of times and scan the area before you decide to ignore the sensation.

You round a corner on the outskirts of town, and you pass by some trashcans. You think that you clear them with plenty of room to spare, but one of them falls over just as you pass. You aren't sure, but you think that you must have hit it. You didn't think that you were *that* bad of a driver.

Not too much further down the road, a screeching cat falls out of a tree right in front of you. You have to swerve to miss hitting it. This has your heart racing and makes you think for a minute about slowing down. Instead, you press on at full speed.

Before going too much further, a tree comes crashing down right behind you on the road. This is too much

18

for coincidence. Someone or something is trying to rattle you, and it is working. You stop your bike and look around again. There is nothing there. You proceed forward again, but much more cautiously this time and at slower speeds.

Soon, you are out on the highway. The sensation of riding your bike at highway speeds is new. It would have been scary enough without everything else going on, but now it is positively terrifying. You are able to keep up with the traffic in the right-hand lane, but vehicles are still passing you. You hope no one will notice that you are driving a smaller hover bike — there isn't too much difference in size between your P11 and the larger P22.

One hover vehicle pulls up beside you with a middle-aged man in it. He looks at you and shakes his head. You think you can read his lips saying, "Phone mode, on." You hope he isn't calling the police.

A couple minutes later, you see it in your mirror–a police hover vehicle is coming up fast. You think, *It is over.* You will be forced to stop this little game of yours, but as the police vehicle gets closer, you realize he is not after you. An older model F-Sunchaser zooms past on the left, and the police vehicle zips by in hot pursuit.

You gaze after the police vehicle, almost wishing he had noticed you so that you could tell him about the note and show him the map. You wrestle in your mind with the thought of going after the police vehicle, but eventually shake off the idea. The urgency of your quest wins the battle.

You are just settling down when you come up behind an antique-looking six-wheel truck driving even more slowly than you are. It is loaded down heavily with old furniture.

You follow behind the truck for a few minutes when suddenly a chair falls off the back end. It comes crashing down on the highway right in front of your hover bike. You slam on the brakes and swerve your bike. You just barely miss it. Instead of startling you, it has a different effect – it makes you mad. *This is enough*, you say to yourself. You could have been killed, and you aren't in the mood to just sit back and play chicken.

There is little traffic to your left right now, so you pull over to the left-hand lane and hit full throttle. You are bound and determined to get a look at the driver of the old truck, but as you speed up, the truck starts going faster. It has amazing pickup for an older vehicle. Soon, it is putting distance between you and itself.

It swerves down an exit without braking and loses some more furniture. You are unable to get over in time to follow it. Your heart is pounding fast, but you are smiling because at least you have done something. You have scored a moral victory.

A few minutes later, you see a sign that says Welcome to Vermont. You are almost there.

The traffic has thinned out, and nothing else happens until you see an exit sign for Mountain Road. The road passes right beside a red barn, too close. It seems like the barn forms a wall for the road. You pass by some cattle grazing near a barbwire fence, and the road winds back into thick woods and makes a steady climb up a mountain.

Before long, the road seems to fade. It blinks in and out and gets narrower. The road, if that's what it is, gives way to a dirt path, which twists back into the woods. You think someone must have used some extraordinary holographic equipment to create an image of a road. Perhaps The Illusionist has technical skills beyond the average scientist and is able to create and hide a road as he wills.

The path narrows, and you are forced to go more slowly. Even though it is sunny, darkness from the

20

dense foliage closes in on you.

You decide to stop to check your map. As you stop, you stare ahead. You think you see a patch of daylight up ahead, but then you realize it isn't coming from the sky. The light seems to be coming from behind some rocks. You pull forward toward the light and see that it is coming up out of the ground.

Chapter Five

The Challenges Begin

You ou stop and lay your bike down behind some pine trees. You half bury it under some pine needles because you are afraid that someone might stumble onto the path and find it. You walk up to the light. You check your map and find that you are at the place that is marked with an "X" by The Illusionist.

You see a hole. You guess the diameter of the hole is three to four feet wide. You can see the bottom when you look down. The hole seems to be about three or four times as deep as you are tall. There is also a rope coming up out of the hole attached to some rocks above the hole. The rope has knots on it. At the top, you can see that they are evenly spaced about every two feet.

You hadn't expected this. Was this some sort of underground hideout? You call down into the hole. "D.D.! Are you down there, D.D.?" The sound of your voice echoes back in your ears. You wait. There is no response, only a dead silence. This makes you notice that the forest all around you seems to be eerily silent as well. The only sound that you can hear now is your own rapid breathing.

Thinking about your sister being held by some madman, you gather up your courage and decide to climb down into the hole. You have a mission to accomplish.

The walls of the hole are wet and muddy. You slip on the wet rope burning your hands. You manage to keep hold, though, because you are in good shape. You think to yourself that you should be able to climb back out too.

When you reach the bottom, you find yourself in a

little room that is about 10 feet wide. It is slippery and muddy. The strange blue light seems to be coming out of some glowing rocks in the ceiling. The room is barely high enough for you to stand up straight.

There is a little hole in the wall at the height of your knees. It is barely big enough to fit in if you stoop down. The passage is as black as a tomb. You are a little scared about going down the small, closed in passage, but you go on, unwaveringly.

You climb into the muddy passage and go about three or four feet in complete darkness when you remember your computer. You can use it as a light source. You say, "Carter, on." The computer comes on in response. You say, "Carter turn up the screen brightness all the way." The screen becomes brighter, giving you a little light to see the passage ahead. You crawl on and soon become glad you are wearing your leather jacket as the cool temperature of the cave settles in on you.

In a few moments, you stumble into a damp room, and a blue light on the ceiling begins glowing. There is a large rock in the middle of the room with a vid-screen attached to it. You can see some writing on the vid-screen. It is a question about grammar.

"So, is this what The Illusionist meant by a challenge?" you ask out loud. "I got you covered. Carter, access grammar disk."

Carter responds, "The disk 081 is blank."

"Blank? What do you mean blank? That's my grammar text."

The computer responds, "The disk 081 is blank."

You figure that The Illusionist, whoever he is, must have cracked the school's security code. The disks are encoded so that the teachers at school can turn them off and on.

You figure that you are out of range for any public

net hookups, but you try anyway. "Carter, hook to the net."

"Network is down or not available."

"Well, what good are you?"

"Please, rephrase the question and ask again."

"Oh, bother. What now?"

You look closer at the grammar question, which reads, "Which part of the following sentence is a simple subject?"

The <u>upstart</u> <u>hero</u> <u>stands</u> ready for the <u>challenge</u>.
    A   B   C   D

There are four keys below the vid-screen marked 'A', 'B', 'C', and 'D'. You decide that you will be able to answer this on your own without the help of your computer. You'll show this Illusionist guy why all your friends call you the *Quiz Kid*. Besides, you don't have much choice.

If you push key 'A', turn to page 111*.
If you push key 'B', turn to page 99*.
If you push key 'C', turn to page 47*.
If you push key 'D', turn to page 151*.

*Remember the page you are on NOW before turning to this page number. See Note to Reader, opposite page 1.

24

"Your brain is even smaller than I thought. It is amazing when you think about it. You humans spend all day learning, and you can't even get a simple grammar question correct."

You want to feel sorry for D.D., but you are having a tough time not feeling sorry for yourself. "What now?" you ask the dragon.

"Well, I'll give you one more chance because the master would want it that way. However, I know you are never going to get it right. Choose the best answer to replace the underlined word or words in the sentence. If the word or words are fine, you may select answer 'D'. Here is the sentence."

Last __and__ not least, pass me and meet your doom!
A) but, B) when, C) because, or D) [No change]

If you tell the dragon 'A', turn to page 111.
If you tell the dragon 'B', turn to page 99.
If you tell the dragon 'C', turn to page 47.
If you tell the dragon 'D', turn to page 151.

"And you wanted to talk to the master? I told you that you would never succeed," says the dragon.

"If you are so smart, why don't you tell me the answer?" you reply.

"Tut, tut, I shall not give the answer away. That is your department. You will simply have to do better. Listen carefully while I give you my next question. You won't get this one wrong if you know what is good for you. Choose the best answer to replace the <u>underlined</u> word or words in the sentence. If the word or words are fine, you may select answer 'D'. Here is the sentence."

You're toast; <u>therefore</u>, I will give you one more chance.
A) however, B) nor, C) even though, or D) [No change]

If you tell the dragon 'A', turn to page 111.
If you tell the dragon 'B', turn to page 99.
If you tell the dragon 'C', turn to page 47.
If you tell the dragon 'D', turn to page 151.

26

The rocks stop glowing. Everything goes black as night.

You take out your computer, and you say, "Carter, on. Turn up your screen brightness all the way." The computer lights up the room.

You go up to the question and read it again. You know that you have gotten the question wrong, and you feel sorry for D.D. You failed the second challenge given to you.

You explore the room a little more, but there isn't much to see. You think about what Mr. Wheatly said, "It may be that you will have more than one chance to rescue your sister." That's when you resign yourself to going back. You go back the way you came and manage to scale the rope back out of the cave.

Turn to page 35.

The dwarves sing out.

"You passed the test;
You are the best.
Now, take this sack,
So you won't lack.
Our good deed,
You will need."

They grab a burlap sack and put a bar of gold from the chest into it. They hand it to you. They then pick you up and put you in another cart on the opposite side of the room. They sing again.

"One last gift we have for you;
You will know what to do."

They hand you a black disk and push you hard in the cart. Out of the room you go and speed down a passageway. The cart dumps you over, and you go through a hole in the floor down a slippery slide.

Turn to page 157.

28

"Hey, Tan, this one is not so bright. I wonder why they calls it the *Quiz Kid?* It should be easy for us to bash its brains," says the goblin on the left. He raises his sword across his body and crouches down.

"You're right, Pan. My sword is ready for some bashing," says Tan as he too raises his sword.

You know that you got the question wrong. You just don't know where your mistake was.

Tan takes a swing at your head with his sword, but you raise your shield in time to deflect the blow. You counter by swiping up with your own blade, and you can feel that it makes contact with the body of the creature.

You look at your sword, and to your surprise, there is a dark red liquid, almost black in color, dripping from your sword. The goblin is holding his side, but he has not fallen yet.

This time, it is Pan who swings wildly at your body. Again, you are able to deflect the blow with your shield, and you strike again, catching him in his face on the cheek. There is more dark red liquid.

You don't wait for them to swing again. You thrust in at Pan, who is holding his cheek, while you duck under another swing from Tan. You catch him full in the belly, and he falls.

Next, you swipe at Tan and catch him with a vicious cut in the body. He too falls at your feet. You begin to feel nauseous, and you wonder if you have just killed. Is this real or an illusion like the road? You are breathing heavily. Your stomach churns, and sweat comes to your face.

Two more equally appalling goblins appear in the doorway. "You beat those two worthless tripe, but you won't beat us." They have their swords ready for battle.

They come at you fast and furious. It is all you can do to beat back their blows. You start losing ground, but there is no place to go. You nick one on the arm, and he slows to put his hand on his wound. This gives you a small chance to concentrate on the other one. You get him on the leg. It is just a scratch, but it is enough.

They are both breathing hard, and they stop coming forward. You are out of breath as well.

"Maybe we gives this one another question," says the goblin on the left.

"Yeah, another question, that's what it needs," says the one on the right. Then, the goblin on the left asks you, "What kind of word is 'arm' in the following sentence?"

You cut me <u>arm</u> with your bloody sword, ouch!
A) adjective, B) article, C) direct object, or D) subject compliment

You think to yourself that you'd like to cut more than its arm, but you concentrate on the question and give this gruesome goblin your answer.

If you answer 'A', turn to page 111.
If you answer 'B', turn to page 99.
If you answer 'C', turn to page 47.
If you answer 'D', turn to page 151.

30

They sing out, "You're not a dud; you could be our bud." They pick you up and put you in a cart on the opposite side of the room. They begin singing.

"Roll, roll, and roll the troll,
Sound the dong, and sound the gong.
Roll, roll, and roll the troll,
Because you won't sing along."

First, they had called you a bud; now, they call you a troll. *Boy, they change their minds fast!* You don't appreciate being called a troll, so you begin to sing, "Dwarves are trolls, with empty heads for bowls."

You are so engulfed in your singing that when you stop, you wind up on your head again.

Turn to page 133.

The computer screen scrolls up with the words, "That is incorrect."

The crystalline woman walks up to you. She says, "Let me ssheee," as she looks at the computer screen. "Ah, I am sssorry. We will have to ssshee if you can do better. Right disssh way." She leads you to a panel on the side of the room. The panel opens, revealing another passage.

You follow her down the passage to another panel, which slides open automatically for her. She says, "Pleassse have a sssheat."

The room is just like the one you had left. There is another crystal figure of a woman typing at a computer on a desk. She appears to not notice you.

There is no furniture in the room besides an empty chair by the entrance. As you go into the room and have a seat in the empty chair, the glass covered panel closes behind you.

After you sit there for what seems to be an eternity, you clear your throat and ask, "Excuse me, do you have a question for me?"

"Pardon me," says the crystal typist. "Pleassse wait a few more minutesss. I am very very busssy today. I have deadliinesss to keep, you know."

You wait longer. After a few minutes, you speak up again. "Can we get on with it?"

The crystalline figure says nothing in responce, and you begin tapping your foot with impatience. After a while, you blurt out, "Ma' am!"

"Okay, okay," she says with a sigh. "Right disssh way." She motions you to sit in the chair in front of the computer, which has an old-fashioned keyboard attached. "Let's ssshee what you can do disssh time." There is a statement on the computer screen that says, "Read the following and find the word that is used incorrectly in the following sentences. Type the correct

32

answer. If there are no mistakes, type selection 'D'."

A) Algae you will remain unless
B) you think more fast. So, think
C) clearly before you're shrimp food.
D) [No mistake.]

If you type 'A', turn to page 111.
If you type 'B', turn to page 99.
If you type 'C', turn to page 47.
If you type 'D', turn to page 151.

"I'm sorry; that was not correct. You will have to do better, or you will not get farther than my stomach."

The dragon continues to sit on top of you and crush you.

"Oh, bother! How can I think with you sitting on top of me? You are going to kill me." You can feel a tightness in your chest, but you know the dragon isn't putting its full weight on top of you. This fact doesn't change your temper. "You can't expect me to think like this!"

"I expect that you simply can't think at all. Well, I suppose we must continue. Listen carefully while I give you my question. Choose the best answer to replace the underlined word or words in the sentence. If the word or words are fine, you may select answer 'D'. Here is the sentence."

Again, I <u>lay</u> on top of the helpless human.
A) lies, B) lie, C) lying, or D) [No change]

If you tell the dragon 'A', turn to page 111.
If you tell the dragon 'B', turn to page 99.
If you tell the dragon 'C', turn to page 47.
If you tell the dragon 'D', turn to page 151.

34

You hand the clipboard back to him. He reads the answer and says, "You can't work for me. You will have to be placcced sssomewhere elssse. I'm sssure you will do fine for sssomeone elssse."

He leads you to a panel on the side of the room, which opens automatically for him. He leads you down another passage to another room. He stays outside while you go into the room.

Turn to page 72.

You are totally dejected, but you did the best you could do.

You decide it will be best if you get your bike and go back home to contact the authorities and bring them back to this spot. You unbury your bike, and you ride back down the path the way you had come. This time, you do not find a road. You follow the path all the way to highway 91.

You have no choice but to go back onto the highway, but you don't stay on the highway very long. You turn off at the first exit.

You pull over at a good spot and get out your computer. "Carter, on," you say. "Bring up a map of Southern Vermont." You are determined to make your way back to your home by the back roads. You aren't going to ride on the highway unless absolutely necessary.

It is getting late, but you make it back to your neighborhood before it gets dark by following the back roads.

As you pull up into your driveway, you notice that there are two extra vehicles in the drive. The outer garage door is shut, so you go around to the side door. The door is locked and isn't responding to your voiceprint. You assume somebody must have turned up the security to maximum. You put your face down to the lock so that it can get a retinal scan of your eye, and you let yourself into the house. Before you get halfway into the kitchen, your mother springs up from her chair and runs over to hug you.

"Oh, one of my dears is home safe," she says. Your father also comes over and gives you a hug. They are a long time in hugging you and fretting over you.

You notice that there are three other men in the room. The one you recognize as Mr. Wheatly.

"Welcome back," he says.

36

"Thank you, Mr. Wheatly."

The other two men then introduce themselves as Agent Parkers and Agent Hanson from the FBI. They want to know all the details of your little trip.

"It is nice to see that you are back. The kidnapping went across state lines so we were brought in," says Agent Parkers. You explain to them everything that happened to you. They are greatly confused because they hadn't been able to find the road, but after hearing everything about the Illusionist, they assume the road was an illusion created by him just for you.

"Don't you worry. We're planning on doing everything within our power to get your sister back," says Agent Hanson.

But you have another plan of your own. You are going straight to your room to study your grammar. You are going to go back to get your sister before they have a chance to find her.

THE END

If you want to go back to try to rescue your sister again, turn to page 21.

"Too bad," they sing out. They come toward you and pick you up with amazing strength. They put you in a cart that rolls on some mini-train tracks. They start singing another song as they push you down a passage.

"Roll along, Roll along,
You didn't pass our test.
Roll along, Roll along,
We think you need some rest."

You thoroughly enjoy your ride as you whiz down a passageway to another room. The cart goes clickety-clack on the track as it rolls along. You don't think that you need a rest, though; you are wide awake. As you whiz into the next room, you can hear a dwarf, dressed in a green suit with a pointed hat, singing this song.

"You were wrong,
You can't move on;
I'll sing my song,
'til you're gone."

The dwarf pulls a lever, stopping the cart. You stay in the cart when it stops. He approaches you and chants, "What is the best way of expressing the idea?"

A) A proper copper cup, works best for a proper cup of coffee.
B) A proper copper cup holds a proper cup of coffee.
C) A proper cup, for a proper cup of coffee, is best.
D) A copper cup holds copper coffee.

If you tell him 'A', turn to page 111.
If you tell him 'B', turn to page 99.
If you tell him 'C', turn to page 47.
If you tell him 'D', turn to page 151.

38

The goblin king says, "You are correct. You know your grammar well. You will march forward far in life, *Quiz Kid.*" The goblin king is standing at his throne now. His hand moves to a button on the arm of the throne. As he pushes it, he begins laughing, and you soon find yourself sliding downward, out of control.

Turn to page 89.

After you answer the question, you hear some grinding and cranking sounds off in the distance.

"Good, it gots it right," says the first goblin. "Now, we can get back to sleep."

"Yeah, back to sleep," says the second goblin.

You are greatly relieved when they drop their swords on the floor. The swords fall with a clang, and the two goblins crawl off back to their rags and fall instantly to sleep.

Turn to page 57.

40

After you answer, you have an uneasy feeling that you have said something wrong. A rock slides open opposite the one you had come through. The vampire turns back into a giant bat. Before you know what is happening, he is upon you, beating his wings against you and clawing you.

You do the best that you can to fend him off, but you are losing ground. You have only one way to go, out the doorway that has just opened. You make your way for the doorway, keeping the bat at bay by swinging your torch.

Turn to page 95.

The man in the coat says, "You ssseem to have made a ssspeedy recovery. You will be able to resssume your normal dutiesss today."

He leads you down a passage to another room that looks like the previous rooms.

Turn to page 93.

42

The crystalline teacher says, "Well, you do ssseem to be having problemsss today. You will need to ssstudy a great deal harder if you want to move up in the world. We will have to come up with an alternative sssstrategy for you. Pleassse follow me."

She leads you out of a panel that opens automatically for her. You follow her out of the room and down a passage to another room. She stays out in the hall as you go into the room.

Turn to page 72.

Feeling pretty certain that you have gotten the qustion right, you run to the next dragon before you become scorched toast.

The dragon is laughing when you arrive. "Ha, I see we have your cooperation," it says. "You would indeed make a fine morsel for our dinner. Perhaps I should just take one of your arms or legs. Then, we would see how fast you could run." It sticks out its forked tongue and licks your leg. "Yummy, a tasty morsel indeed."

"I'd like to keep both my arms and legs, thank you. Do you have a question for me?" you ask in response.

"Yes, a question, but I doubt that you will get it; you don't seem too bright. If you get it wrong, perhaps then we will eat you. Listen carefully to my question. Choose the best answer to replace the underlined word or words in the sentence. If the word or words are fine, you may select answer 'D'. Here is the sentence."

By flossing with your leg, I can prevent tooth decay. A) flossing, B) After flossing, C) In case flossing, or D) [No change]

If you tell the dragon 'A', turn to page 111.
If you tell the dragon 'B', turn to page 99.
If you tell the dragon 'C', turn to page 47.
If you tell the dragon 'D', turn to page 151.

44

"You won't be moving up in the world with answersss like that. You won't pull a fassst one on me. I tell you what I'm going to do. I'm going to let you ssspeak to my partner."

He leads you to a panel on the side of the room. The panel opens up for him automatically. He leads you down a passage to another room. He waits outside while you go into the room.

In the room is another desk and chair like the previous room. Sitting at the desk is another glass crystal figure of a man wearing a very wide, icicle-shaped, maroon tie. Down the center of his tie is a picture of a fish skeleton.

When you enter the room, he gets up from his desk. He comes over to the other side of his desk and leans back on the desk. "Ssso, my partner wasssn't sssatisfied with your performanccce, *Quiz Kid*, and now it isssh up to me. Let'sss ssshee what we can do. I will have to asssk you a quessstion too."

He goes around the desk and gets out a hand-held computer much like your own. He gives it to you to use. "Computer, on," you say. "Display the question." On its screen, you read, "What word is used <u>incorrectly</u> in the following sentences? Select the correct answer. If there are no mistakes, choose selection 'D'."

A) *Not nobody can see with ink*
B) *in their eyes. So answering this*
C) *question will let you see your way.*
D) *[No mistake.]*

If you answer 'A', turn to page 111.
If you answer 'B', turn to page 99.
If you answer 'C', turn to page 47.
If you answer 'D', turn to page 151.

After you write your answer, the rock that had slid aside between you and the skeletons slides back open. This lets the three skeletons scramble into the room. There is nowhere to go. You have to fight them.

After several parries and thrusts and much wild swinging, you find your mark on one of the attacking skeletons. You hit it in the chest with your torch, and it catches on fire, burning bright and quick. Soon after realizing how to destroy them, you have the other two in ashes upon the ground.

You know the skeletons can't be real, but this still makes you feel uneasy.

When the third one falls, a sliding rock reveals another passageway out of the room. Another thick dust cloud forms as before. You proceed down the passage through the dust and smoke into another room that is similar to the first one.

Three ghastly skeletons stand abreast with daggers in hand, and another old-fashioned parchment sits on a wooden table as before. This time you waste no time; you read and follow the instructions on the parchment right away. "Choose the best answer to fill in the <u>blank</u> in the sentence below."

Only the _____ defeats the undead.
A) swifter, B) more swift, C) most swift, or D) swiftest

Holding the torch, you take the quill pen in your free hand, dip it in the inkbottle, and write your answer.

If you write 'A', turn to page 111.
If you write 'B', turn to page 99.
If you write 'C', turn to page 47.
If you write 'D', turn to page 151.

46

He sings out, "You are grand at grammar. This could be your finest hour." He pulls the lever, which switches the tracks on the floor, and then he gives the cart a great heave. He sings as you roll along.

"Push the cart,
On the track.
Sing this song,
And don't look back."

Turn to page 113.

From page 23, turn to 83.
From page 24, turn to 132.
From page 25, turn to 121.
From page 29, turn to 134.
From page 32, turn to 141.
From page 33, turn to 59.
From page 37, turn to 97.
From page 43, turn to 78.
From page 44, turn to 80.
From page 45, turn to 74.
From page 50, turn to 37.
From page 54, turn to 45.
From page 56, turn to 120.
From page 57, turn to 152.
From page 58, turn to 26.
From page 74, turn to 127.
From page 76, turn to 34.
From page 78, turn to 165.
From page 79, turn to 169.
From page 82, turn to 149.
From page 86, turn to 100.
From page 87, turn to 77.
From page 91, turn to 31.
From page 94, turn to 130.
From page 100, turn to 138.
From page 104, turn to 109.
From page 106, turn to 108.

From page 107, turn to 162.
From page 109, turn to 135.
From page 114, turn to 145.
From page 115, turn to 107.
From page 117, turn to 101.
From page 119, turn to 38.
From page 123, turn to 118.
From page 125, turn to 85.
From page 126, turn to 87.
From page 127, turn to 109.
From page 129, turn to 28.
From page 131, turn to 42.
From page 133, turn to 27.
From page 137, turn to 76.
From page 140, turn to 149.
From page 142, turn to 74.
From page 144, turn to 166.
From page 145, turn to 97.
From page 148, turn to 54.
From page 153, turn to 75.
From page 155, turn to 71.
From page 159, turn to 163.
From page 161, turn to 40.
From page 164, turn to 25.
From page 165, turn to 24.
From page 171, turn to 97.

Chapter Nine
Jolly Men

The cave you find yourself in is larger than any
room you've encountered so far. This chamber has many
smaller caves connected to it. Some of these smaller
caves have mini-train tracks in them while others
contain only pathways. On the tracks are metal carts
trimmed in wood. Though the chamber is a work in
progress, it gives the appearance of orderliness and
neatness.

You see two funny little men, dwarves by their look
and dress, chipping away with pick axes at the far wall.
Their muscular arms bulge out of rolled-up sleeves, and
they have rosy cheeks and long beards. The green suits
that they're wearing remind you of Robin Hood's merry
men, especially of the rotund Friar Tuck. Only, instead
of hoods, they wear pointed hats that droop over
backward.

They have some tools neatly lined up behind them:
shovels, axes, sieves, and various other instruments
which you don't recognize. A pile of rocks stands behind
them like a pyramid. They have small lanterns for light,
and a massive lantern hangs from the ceiling. The
rhythmic sound their picks make as they work rings
out in harmony to the song they sing.

"We work all day; we work all night;
Happy with the toilsome plight.
We never stop; we never rest,
To gather copper for our chest."

The dwarves have pleasant, hearty, singing voices,
which you enjoy. When they finish their song, they put

down their picks and turn toward you. They join arm-in-arm and dance over to you. They sing the same tune with a, "Da da do and a la la lou. Hello, *Quiz Kid*. Here's a grammar question just for you." As one, they chant, "Which is the best way of expressing the idea?"

A) *Dwarves, happy workers, seek copper for their chest.*
B) *Dwarves are happy workers who seek copper for their chest.*
C) *Happy dwarves, who seek copper for their chest, are workers.*
D) *Happy dwarves are workers who seek copper for their chest.*

You smile and answer their question.

If you tell them 'A', turn to page 111.
If you tell them 'B', turn to page 99.
If you tell them 'C', turn to page 47.
If you tell them 'D', turn to page 151.

51

After you write the letter, you have an uneasy feeling that you have done something wrong. This time, two rock panels slide open at the same time. The first rock panel that opens is the one you just came through. The second panel is across the room directly opposite the first. The skeletons scramble into the room. Before you know what is happening, they are upon you, swinging their daggers and grabbing for you.

You do your best to fend them off, but you are losing ground. You have only one way to go, and that is out the second doorway. You make your way for the doorway, keeping the skeletons at bay.

Turn to page 95.

52

"You are a very adept student of language, *Quiz Kid*. Vould you care for something to eat?"

You answer, "No. No, thank you."

"Perhaps, you vouldn't mind it if I had a bite myself," says the man as he gets out of his coffin and comes a little closer to you.

Thinking that you may be the main course he has in mind, you respond with an emphatic, "Yes. Yes, I would mind. Where are you hiding my sister?"

"I see," says the vampire, "Perhaps, we can share a drink." He produces a glass canter with red liquid in it and two glasses. He pours the liquid into the glasses and hands one to you.

You take the glass and smell the liquid as the man takes his and quickly drinks it. The scent of the dark red liquid makes your stomach do a somersault.

"No, thank you. I'd prefer to not drink anything," you say as you throw the glass down to the floor.

Before it hits the ground, the vampire swoops down and catches the glass laughing, "Never vaste guud blood my fiend, never." His speed amazes you, and you begin to get a little frightened. You think you may end up having to fight him, but he seems much too fast.

He seems to sense your fear for he coos, "Do not vorry, my fiend," and he claps twice. A door opens up behind his coffin. "You may prroceed."

You walk past the vampire and through the door. You walk down a passage behind the doorway into a small room with a small stone table in the middle of it. On the table sits a little black disk. Putting the disk into your computer, you say, "Carter, on. Read the disk."

"Very good. You have made it through the *Hall of the Undead*. Welcome to the *Mining Facilities*."

The floor opens up, and you slide down again.

Turn to page 49.

The crystalline teacher-figure leads you to another panel door that leads down another hall. At the end of the hall, another room opens before you. At the direction of the teacher, you go in. She stays out in the hall.

There is nothing in the room except a disk. You put the disk into your computer. "Carter, on. Read the disk," you say.

"Congratulations, *Quiz Kid,* you have made it through Aqua Land. Welcome to the Hall of the Undead."

Suddenly, the floor gives out below you, and you fall through a trap door.

Turn to page 147.

54

After you write the letter, a passageway opens on the left side of the room. You are pretty unsure of your answer — maybe you did something wrong. As you are thinking, you hear clinking noises. The three skeletons seem to be alive, something is animating them, and they are coming at you. You take your torch in hand and fend them off as best you can.

"Stay back!" you yell. "Get away from me." You think, *This can't be real; it is like something out of a horror movie-vid.*

The three skeletons are swinging their daggers at you and reaching for you with the claws of their free hands. The battle with them gives you the chills. You are slowly being forced back.

You make your way toward the door that had opened up before. At the doorway, you are able to hold them at bay. Eventually, you are able to move into the room. As you enter, a rock slides back into place, closing up the opening between you and the skeletons.

You examine the room for the first time. The space is empty except for a wooden table on which there is another parchment, ink bottle, and quill pen. This time, you think to yourself that you will do better on your answer. You read the instruction, "Choose the best answer to fill in the <u>blank</u> in the sentence below."

The way to prosper is by _____ the answer correctly.
A) to write, B) write, C) writing, or D) written

Holding the torch, you take the quill pen in your free hand, dip it, and write your answer.

If you write 'A', turn to page 111.
If you write 'B', turn to page 99.
If you write 'C', turn to page 47.
If you write 'D', turn to page 151.

"You are correct. You may proceed," concede the dragons. They all slither away, back into the cave.

You make your way across the chamber to stand before the largest dragon you have yet encountered. It is still asleep on a small hill of gold. Narrowly opening its eyes when you arrive, she asks, "Ah, *Quiz Kid*. Have you met my children? Oh yes, I see from the fire marks on the back of your jacket that you have. You think I will let you go through? Perhaps, I will, but also perhaps, I will change my mind. I don't always listen to directions. As you can see, I am much older and larger than my children are. You wouldn't even make a good snack for me, you are so small. Maybe I can be persuaded to ask you a question. Most people who visit me bring me a gift. Do you have something for me?"

"I have this," you say, handing her the brick of gold that you got from the dwarves. You are hoping that she, too, will listen to the master whoever that is.

"This is a very fine piece of gold indeed. I think I will allow you to live. That is if you can answer my question. Listen most carefully. Which <u>one</u> of the following stories would be most appropriate in a report on dragons?"

A) Throughout time, there have been many mythical creatures. Dragons are mythical creatures like pixies, elves, and even gnomes. In one myth, it was written that if you knew the name of a dragon, you would have power over it.

B) Dragons are creatures from myth that have been claimed to be large, terrible lizards. They have large, taloned claws and thick, rough, scaly hides. Lizards don't breath fire; dragons do. However, not all dragons from myth breathe fire, and some lizards squirt chemicals from their heads.

C) Legend states that dragons are majestic creatures. Dragons are said to possess many gifts. Some

56

reported gifts are the power of flight, the skill to breath fire from their mouths, and the capability to read a weaker being's mind. Whether these facts are true or not, dragons certainly have the power to capture our imagination and pique our curiosity.

D) A dragon legend, which seems to be universal, is their love for treasure and fine things. Dragons love gold, silver, and shiny objects. They even horde and collect this treasure, stacking it in their lairs.

It is hard to concentrate in the presence of such a large and terrifying dragon, but you do your best.

If you tell the dragon 'A', turn to page 111.
If you tell the dragon 'B', turn to page 99.
If you tell the dragon 'C', turn to page 47.
If you tell the dragon 'D', turn to page 151.

You turn and go out of the room, down to where the two passages split. This time, you choose the passage on the left.

You enter a room just like the one you just left. There are two more goblins sound asleep on a pile of dirty, old rags.

This must be what these disgusting creatures call bedrooms, you think. "Yuck!"

As before, nailed onto the farthest wall is an antique-looking parchment on which there is some writing. This time, the message says, "What part of speech is the word 'were' in the following sentence?"

The goblins <u>were</u> asleep, dreaming of tasty sheep.
A) adverb, B) linking verb, C) gerund, or D) adjective

Below the parchment, on the rock wall are some mini-switches marked 'A', 'B', 'C', and 'D'. Even though you really want to get out of this disgusting room, you take the time to mull over the possible choices. You finally select an answer and activate a mini-switch.

If you select 'A', turn to page 111.
If you select 'B', turn to page 99.
If you select 'C', turn to page 47.
If you select 'D', turn to page 151.

58

The vid-screen lights up. "Correct," it says.

You hear some grinding sounds, and the cave begins to shake. Something makes a loud bang, and one of the walls in the room falls backward and crashes. The hole made by the fallen wall opens up another passageway.

The passageway is larger and drier than the previous one, but it seems to be made of the same kind of rock as the rest of the passages you have encountered. The floor seems to be smoother, however.

You walk down the new passage using your computer for light again. You come to another room much like the one you have just left. This room has the same kind of blue light glowing from the ceiling. A thin, rock slab is set up against the far wall. You make your way toward the slab and notice a message engraved on its face. You read the message aloud, "Which part of the following sentence is a simple subject?"

The <u>challenge</u> involves <u>battle</u> with <u>forces</u> of <u>many</u> kinds.　　A　　　　　B　　　　C　　　D

Your eyes shift their gaze and rest on four rock knobs beneath the engraving. After thinking briefly, you make your selection and turn one of the knobs.

If you turn knob 'A', turn to page 111.
If you turn knob 'B', turn to page 99.
If you turn knob 'C', turn to page 47.
If you turn knob 'D', turn to page 151.

"Wrong again," the dragon says as he gets off of you. "You are indeed not worthy of getting your sister. I will count to three before I breathe fire on you."

You do the only thing that seems prudent—you run. You run back the way you had come. This time, there is no barrier blocking your exit. You run back to the safety of your narrow passage and little room. As you come around a bend, fire comes flowing into the passage, heating your back.

Turn to page 167.

60

The crystalline nurse says, "Ok, your mind isssh working jussst fine. You can resssume your regular dutiesss today. Right disssh way."

She leads you across the room to a panel on the far wall. The panel slides open, revealing a hall. At the end of the hall is another room like the previous rooms.

Turn to page 93.

Chapter Eleven
The Great Escape

You find yourself sitting on a smooth, cool floor, surrounded by darkness. You grab your computer and say, "Carter, on. Turn up the brightness." The computer lights up enough to let you see that you are in a small, circular, natural cavern. There is only one exit from the cavern that you can see.

You cautiously go through the exit and proceed down a passageway, which ends at a tunnel. You can see a dim light at the end of the tunnel, and you want to surprise whoever or whatever might be there, so you whisper, "Carter, off."

After traveling through the tunnel, you carefully enter a room. The floor is neatly covered in black and white tiles. There is a control console in the room. The console and the walls are equipped with several vid-screens and are full of buttons, switches, and knobs. On the far wall are five chairs with a person sitting in the middle one. The person is fastened to the chair with metal straps, and a virtual-helmet covers his head. You aren't sure, but you think the person is wearing D.D.'s clothes. It must be D.D.!

Behind the console is a man whose age you guess to be thirty-something. His wavy, black hair is neatly groomed, and he is closely shaved. He wears a purple cape decorated with small, white stars and moons, purple pants with black, silk stripes down the sides, and a white, ruffled "tux" shirt.

"Come in, please. I have been expecting you. You have done very well indeed, *Quiz Kid.* I hope you liked all my little illusions," he says with a crooked grin on his face as he stares at you.

62

"So, do I finally get to meet The Illusionist face to face?" you ask as you step into the room.

"Ha, do I sense a note of temper in your voice?"

"I'm not angry. I am just curious. Do you get your jollies out of testing young people and kidnapping their sisters?"

"I'm not surprised that you'd like to know for what end I do these things. But you are not in a position to demand anything, so I choose not to tell you," he answers.

You walk closer to him. In truth, your temper is up, and you think seriously of trying to fight this madman. But, instead, you control your temper and say, "I assume I have passed all your little tests. Are you going to free my sister now?"

"Your sister will be freed when I am good and ready and not before. You know you really are quite intelligent, *Quiz Kid*. I see a great future for you if you will just allow yourself to be guided by the right mentor."

"Well, thank you for the compliment. And whom do you have in mind? Surely, not yourself."

"There would be many benefits to working with me. You could do worse, much worse."

"I wouldn't work for you in a million years, Bud."

"Pity. You may change your mind–after time. Well, I'll let you think about it for a while." He pulls his cape around himself and disappears in a puff of shimmering smoke.

You run into the room up to D.D. and call out, "D.D., D.D., are you OK?" You try to get the straps off her arms and remove the virtual-helmet from her head, but they won't budge. "Don't worry D.D., I'll get you loose. Just hang on."

But as you are leaning over, you start to cough and feel dizzy. A cloud of dense fog begins to rise from the floor. "Uh, what is this? More trickery? It must be sleeping gas." You gasp for air and struggle against it for a few seconds before you black out.

When you come to, you are sitting in a chair. Your hands and feet are restrained, and you see nothing but blackness. You try moving your head, but it is restrained. You realize that you must also be wearing a virtual-helmet. You think you must be sitting in one of the chairs next to your sister D.D.

After sitting in blackness for a few minutes, you hear a voice. "I see that the effects of the sleeping gas have worn off. You really should make this easy on yourself and at least consider my proposal."

"You'll never get away with this. The police will find you."

"Such a cliché. The police can't find their nose to spite their face. There is no one who can help you, *Kid*. No one is capable of matching my powers."

"Even if no one does find me, I will never follow you."

"Don't be so sure about that. Pleasant dreams."

Suddenly, you're having visions. You see D.D. riding her horse at your neighbor's, the Mick's. She is jumping over some gates and laughing. You are leaning on a fence smiling to yourself. She seems to be doing very well. Suddenly, she takes a fall. You climb the fence and run over to her as fast as you can. You fall face down in a puddle of dirty water on the way. "D.D.! Are you alright, D.D.?" She isn't moving.

The vision suddenly changes. You are in your house walking up the stairs to your parents' bedroom. You walk up the first three stairs to the landing. Suddenly, the stairs start lifting up, rising and falling. Holding on to the wall to maintain your balance, you call out to your parents, but your voice won't rise above a whisper.

The vision quickly changes again. This time, you are in a rowboat on a body of water; it looks like the bay.

64

The day is extremely hot, and the sun beats down on your head, making you sweat. The water is choppy, violently rocking the boat. Your stomach churns, and you feel like you are going to be sick.

The sick feeling doesn't last long. You think you are still dreaming, but somehow the dream seems different. You can see yourself and D.D. trapped in The Illusionist's room, strapped to chairs, but the vision is blurry.

"Don't worry. I'll have you out in a second." Your virtual-helmet is removed, and the dream stops immediately. You realize it is the helmet that made you see the visions, another trick of The Illusionist. You see a person standing over you, wearing a hood, which covers his entire head. The only thing you can see are his intense, dark blue eyes peering out of the eye slots in the hood. "I was sent by a friend," says the hooded figure. In his hand, he holds an instrument, and he is working to release your arm straps. Before long, he has both of your hands free, and he starts on your ankles.

"Who are you?" you ask.

"I already told you that a friend sent me. Please, we don't have much time; it took us quite a while to find you. We were able to scramble The Illusionist's network, but it won't take him long to get back online."

When both your legs are freed, the hooded figure starts working on D.D.'s restraints. Before long, she is free as well.

"Oh, D.D., I am so happy to see you." You pull her close and hug her.

"I am happy to see you, too. I was having such strange dreams. I dreamt that you were in a dungeon fighting all these terrible monsters. You were trying to save me, but you couldn't get to me."

"That wasn't a dream. The virtual-helmet you were wearing let you see everything."

"How are we going to get out of here, and who is this person?"

"I am a friend. Now, will you two please follow me, quickly?"

The hooded figure goes over to the control console and types on a computer keyboard. On the opposite side of the room, a secret wall panel pivots open. He hurries to the secret panel and goes through it with you and D.D. following right behind.

The hooded figure leads you down a long corridor that looks like it belongs in an office building. On both sides of the corridor are doors every few yards, and at regular intervals, the hallway intersects with other corridors. Before long, you come to a door that is different. "Door open," says the hooded figure. In obedience to the voice command, the door slides aside with a hiss.

The hooded figure goes into the small compartment with you and D.D. "Second level," he bellows into a speaker grill on the wall. The door to the compartment closes, and you feel the room begin to move at a rapid speed, which makes your stomach flutter. You realize you are on an elevator.

As the elevator is traveling, your curiosity gets the best of you, and you ask, "Who sent you?"

"I can't tell you that. You will have to be satisfied that you are being helped for now and leave it at that."

"Well, thank you very much," says D.D. with a bright smile.

"You're quite welcome," the hooded figure replies, smiling beneath his hood.

The elevator comes to a stop, and the door hisses open. You walk down several corridors, passing many more doors, before you finally halt in front of one. This door looks just like all the rest to you, but the hooded figure opens it by waving his hand. Beyond the door is a small office with a desk, other office furniture, and a window. Outside the window, it is as dark as night. You've lost all track of time in The Illusionist's hideout. You think it is a little early for nighttime, though.

"This way," says the hooded figure as he leads you to the window. He opens it and climbs out, switching on something in a cone-shaped case that looks like a light bulb, only brighter. The light device has a strap on it, which he wraps around his head. From the light's beam, you can see that he is standing in a natural cave. You and D.D. climb out of the window and join him. He leads you through the cave.

You walk for several minutes, climbing part of the way. Shortly, you are out of the cave and standing in daylight in the middle of a wooded area. The bright sun makes your eyes water. You walk through woods for a while until you come to a pathway. "Your bike is in this direction. Come on, hurry," the hooded figure says as he leads you up the path.

"Shouldn't we call the police?" you ask.

"We don't work with the police very much," responds the hooded figure.

"Yeah, but shouldn't The Illusionist pay for his crime?"

"You are welcome to call the police if you like. But I doubt that they will be able to find The Illusionist's network, much less scramble it. With his network running, they will never be able to make their way inside his vast, cavernous hideout. The only way we could navigate through the caverns was by running our own little deception program on top of his network. The illusions were never gone; the images were just changed a little. Besides, I doubt The Illusionist is even there. He is probably managing the whole operation from a remote location, using a hologram to make you think he's in the cave. That's what I would do."

Soon, you come to the pine grove where you had hidden your bike. The hooded figure stops. "Now, where is your hover bike?"

"Over here," you say excitedly. You run past him hurriedly to your bike with D.D. following quickly behind. You start the motor, and when you turn around, the hooded figure is gone. Suddenly, a large raven flies into the sky above you and D.D. Circling, the raven looks down at you and makes a deep resonant "kaw" sound as it speeds away.

You look up, watching the bird, shielding your eyes from the sun, and say, "We didn't even get a chance to say good-bye."

With D.D. on the back of the hover bike, you follow the path out of the pine grove. This time, there is no road. The path leads you to highway 91.

You go much more slowly this time, but before long you are back home. While driving up your driveway, you notice that both of your parents' vehicles are in the garage, but two strange vehicles are parked in the driveway as well.

After parking your hover bike, you go inside the garage. But you can't get in the house because the inside garage door is locked. The lock will not respond to your voiceprint. So, you suppose that someone must have changed the code on the security system. You put your face near the lock to let it get a retinal scan from your eye. The door opens, and you and D.D. enter the house. You think to yourself, *There really is no place like home.*

As you walk into the kitchen, your mother springs from her chair. Tears are rolling down her cheeks as she runs towards you and D.D. She nearly smothers you and D.D. with hugs. Then, your father joins in the celebration too, and you have one big group hug.

After a while, you notice that there are three men in the kitchen. You recognize Mr. Wheatly, but the other

68

two men are strangers. They introduce themselves as Agent Parkers and Agent Hanson from the FBI.

"FBI, wow!" you say. "How do we warrant the FBI?"

"The kidnapping went across state lines, so we were called," says agent Parkers. "It is nice to see that you two are back. What happened?"

Sitting at the table with a nice cup of hot chocolate, you explain to them everything that had happened. They are greatly confused because earlier they couldn't find the road that you describe. After hearing everything about The Illusionist, however, they assume that the road must have been an illusion that he had created just for you.

"We will be working to find that network and shut down that little operation," says agent Hanson.

"It worked out fine for you, didn't it?" Mr. Wheatly asks you with a twinkle in his eyes and a tight-lipped smile on his face.

"Yes, yes it did Mr. Wheatly," you respond with a quizzical look.

The next morning you awake from a good night's sleep. Stretching and yawning, you get out of bed. Not knowing what to do with yourself since your parents gave you the day off from school, you decide to check your email messages. You stretch again and make your way to your desk.

"Carter, on. Show incoming email messages."

As you scan the screen, you realize that you haven't deleted the old messages. Your eyes focus on the one from D.D. It still screams, "HORSES ARE THE BEST." This brings a crooked smile to your face as you slowly shake your head.

Before deleting the message, you take Carter next door to show your sister. As you walk into her room, you see her riding boots on the floor with the chair still out in the middle, close to the boots. D.D. is not in her room.

As you quickly look around, inspecting the bedroom, you feel yourself getting dizzy. Your head starts to ache, and you have to sit down. As you raise your hand to your forehead, you feel a large lump, which you assume was caused from hitting your head on the chair the day before. You start to wonder if all the recent events had just been a bad dream.

Suddenly Carter announces, "You have mail." You glance at the computer screen and see a new message entitled "Good Morning, Sunshine." There is no name for the sender.

"Carter, show the 'Good Morning' message." You read it.

"Good Morning,
 I sincerely hope you got a good night's sleep. I trust you don't think that the little man who freed you from my place was really your friend. He was just another one of my little tricks. I will see you again very soon. You can be sure of that! — The Illusionist"

THE END

70

The man with no face starts laughing in his deep, husky voice. He says, "You got it wrong."

Suddenly, he vanishes, and his laughing stops as blackness fills the room. You take out your computer and say, "Carter, on. Turn up the screen brightness all the way." The computer lights up the room.

As you look around, there is nothing there. The man is gone, along with the chair. After exploring the room for a while, you think about what Mr. Wheatly had said, "It may be that you will have more than one chance to rescue your sister." That's when you resign yourself to going back the way you had come. You manage to scale the rope out of the cave.

Turn to page 35.

They sing again, "You got it wrong my friend; now your time must end." The one in the middle starts blowing a sad dirge sound on the jug. One of the dwarves walks over and pulls a lever on the floor. The third dwarf comes up to the cart and pushes it.

Turn to page 97.

There is nothing in the room. You find yourself staring and blinking at blank walls.

After standing there for a while, contemplating your next move, you hear a strange sound coming from behind the walls. Then, little holes open in the ceiling, and torrents of water start to gush into the room.

Soon, you are standing in a foot of water. You start to yell, "Someone please let me out of here!" over and over. Your voice grows hoarse. You start banging on the walls to no avail. Nothing seems to work. The water continues to rise steadily.

Soon, the water rises to your waist. Concerned that your computer might get damaged, you take it out of your pouch and command, "Carter. Watertight mode on." The computer immediately encases itself in a seamless covering.

Right after you do this, a panel in the wall opens. The water gushes out, pulling you with it. You lose your balance, slipping out and down a long, dark slide inside of a cave.

After a while, the water pressure ceases, and you stop sliding. You are soaked. The cave is dark, and you can't see anything. You remember your computer. "Carter, watertight mode off. Activate visual mode." You command, "Turn up the brightness all the way." You sit up and look around. You are in the middle of a dark cave that slopes down. The water is running beneath you in a trickle now.

You get up and follow the contour of the cave. Eventually, the cave empties out into a wooded area with a small stream. You follow the course of the stream for a while until you come to a trail. The trail goes east and west.

Since you remember being at a high elevation when you entered the cave, you follow the trail west, which takes you in an upward direction. After walking for about

30 minutes, you come to the pine trees where you had buried your bike. This time, there is no blue light, but you recognize the rocks. You walk up to the hole, but there is no rope coming up out of the hole.

Turn to page 35.

74

After you write your answer, a passageway opens on one side of the room. You are quite unsure of your answers. Maybe you did something wrong. As you are thinking, you hear clinking noises as before. The three skeletons are coming at you. You take your torch in hand and fend them off as best you can.

You think that you will just burn them like before, but this proves a little more difficult. They are fighting you better and won't let you get a clean shot at them.

The three skeletons are swinging their daggers at you and reaching for you with their free hands. You are forced back.

You make your way for the door that had opened up for you. You are able to hold them back at the doorway. Eventually, you go into the room. As you go in, a rock slides back into place between you and the skeletons.

You examine the room for the first time. The room is empty except for a wooden table with another parchment, inkbottle, and quill pen. This time, you think to yourself that you will do better on your answer. You read the instruction, "Choose the best answer to fill in the <u>blank</u> in the sentence below."

You will _____ your end if you fail to answer correctly.

A) meat, B) met, C) meet, or D) meets

Holding the torch, you take the quill pen in your free hand, dip it in the inkbottle, and write your answer.

If you write 'A', turn to page 111.
If you write 'B', turn to page 99.
If you write 'C', turn to page 47.
If you write 'D', turn to page 151.

Lan says, "Now, we gets to beat it."

Wan agrees, "Yeah, and eats it too. Yum, Yum goes the dumb, dumb."

They had barely let up from their attack to ask you questions, and now they are back at it in full fury. It is all you can do to deflect their blows. Soon, they force you back the way you had come. You are losing ground rapidly.

The repeated blows force you back into the room where you had fallen through the trap door. It is a mess, and you can't navigate through all the fallen goblins. Wan gives you a hard shove against your shield sending you sprawling backwards as you trip over a body. You hit your head against the hard floor and slide into the wall. Only instead of finding a wall to stop your momentum, you go straight through.

Turn to page 170.

76

The iceman takes the clipboard back from you. He reads your answer and scratches his head. He says, "Well, we may have another placcce for you. You can't work for me; that'sss for sssure."

He leads you to a panel in the side of the room. The panel opens up for him.

He leads you down a passage into another room. He stays outside while you go into the room. There is another figure of a man standing in the corner, holding a clipboard, and wearing a hat. You can still hear the sounds of construction in the background.

The man comes up to you. "Let'sss sssshee; we need to sssshee where we can placcce you. Have a look at thisss, and ansssswer the quesssstion. It will help usss sssshee where you belong."

He hands you the clipboard. Again, it has digi-paper and an electric pen on it. You take it and read the question. "What word is used <u>incorrectly</u> in the following sentences? Mark the correct answer. If there are no mistakes, mark selection 'D'."

A) I know I can dunk on your
B) head, you little shrimp, so let's you
C) and I play some one-on-one.
D) [No mistake.]

It seems simple enough, and you immediately mark down your answer.

If you write down 'A', turn to page 111.
If you write down 'B', turn to page 99.
If you write down 'C', turn to page 47.
If you write down 'D', turn to page 151.

"I see," says the dragon. "I see that you are wrong again. Now, it is time for our conversation to end. You must go before I roast you alive. I will give you a sporting chance for a head start."

You don't need to hear it twice. You know that your time with the dragon is through. You also know that you would never make it past him, so you do the only thing that you can do. You run back the way that you had come. This time, there is no invisible barrier blocking your way. You are very thankful for this fact.

You make it back into the passage and think you are safe, but you can feel the heat from the dragon's breath on your back.

Turn to page 167.

"Ha, ha, ha. I knew you wouldn't get it. Perhaps we will eat you." He sticks out his forked tongue and licks you again.

This makes you feel absolutely gross. You say, "Do you have another question for me, or what?"

"Yes, the master would have me give you one more chance. But after that, it is dinnertime, and you are mine. Listen carefully to my question. Choose the best answer to replace the <u>underlined</u> word or words in the sentence. If the word or words are fine, you may select answer 'D'. Here is the sentence."

You <u>discovered</u> my fiery heat if you answer this incorrectly.

A) discovers, B) have discovered, C) will discover, or D) [No change]

You are having a tough time concentrating with the dragon's head so close to you, but you do the best that you can.

If you tell the dragon 'A', turn to page 111.
If you tell the dragon 'B', turn to page 99.
If you tell the dragon 'C', turn to page 47.
If you tell the dragon 'D', turn to page 151.

"No, pea brain. That wasn't the correct answer," says the goblin king. "Now I has a surprise for you." He puts a couple of fingers in his mouth and whistles loudly.

You stand there, dumbfounded, as two spears leave the wall by themselves and come flying at you. It is all you can do to fend off the two soaring spears.

"What kind of trickery is this?" you scream as you hack and hack at the spears. But every time you beat them down, they just repeat their assault. You fight on bravely for several minutes until you start to get very tired.

The goblin king laughs and says, "I'll gives you another question, and if you answers it good, I'll release you. He whistles again, and the wicked spears drop lifelessly to the ground. As before, he hands you a dirty piece of old parchment and tells you, "Read this." On the parchment is written, "Read the following paragraph. Choose the sentence that does not belong in the paragraph below."

(1) On your 6th birthday, your Buddy Doll fell into the pool and short-circuited. (2) When you were ten, at Christmas time, Lucy the cat knocked over the tree, and you were blamed. (3) You received a brand new hover sled, but you crashed into a tree on the same day. (4) In the battle with the Goblin King, as the spears attacked, you felt all was lost.

A) sentence 1, B) sentence 2, C) sentence 3, or D) sentence 4

If you answer 'A', turn to page 111.
If you answer 'B', turn to page 99.
If you answer 'C', turn to page 47.
If you answer 'D', turn to page 151.

80

After you answer, he says, "Yesssh, I sssee. We do have a problem here. You will have to find a placcce elsssewhere. You do not ssseem to have what it takesss to make it here. Pleassse follow me, would you?"

He leads you to a side panel in the room. The panel opens automatically for him. He leads you down another passage to another room. He stays outside while you go into the room.

Turn to page 72.

When you finish writing your answer, the three coffins open and out come three grizzly specters. Walking corpses — animated mummies — are moving in your direction. They have their arms out, and they are moaning a dreadful groan. You hold your torch up and swing it from side to side to keep them at bay, but they still come forward. The closer they get, the louder they groan. The louder they groan, the more they frighten you.

Finally, your torch catches one of them on fire. He burns more slowly than the skeletons and makes a lot of thick, black smoke. It continues moving for a little while as it burns. Next, you have the second one burning and then the third. By the time you are done, you are coughing up a storm from all of the smoke. The smoke gives off an offensive odor as well and makes you want to lose your lunch.

A grinding noise becomes perceptible by your ear despite your coughing. The coffin on the far wall slides aside revealing a passageway behind it. You follow it out quickly to escape from the smoke.

You go down a much longer passage into another room. This room is as large as the one with the mummies. The room has a table with a coffin lying flat on the floor behind it. The coffin is not old like the previous three you had encountered; it is shiny and new. It has ornate gold lettering around the sides of it in a language you can't read.

When you look up, at first glance, the ceiling seems to be alive. Upon closer inspection, you realize that the ceiling is covered with bats.

You hate bats. They always give you the creeps. But you bravely go up to the table and read the parchment that is lying upon the table. It contains this instruction, "Choose the sentence that best completes the paragraph below."

"Let me tell you a story," the vampire began. *"Long ago, I lived in a country named Transylvania. I was an ordinary human like you, but in one fateful day I was changed forever. While I slept at night, a huge, black bat bit me on the neck. _____. For thousands of years since that terrible night, I have been a vampire, eternally cursed to darkness."*

A) My homeland had many mountains, and I loved to explore them.

B)The bat flew to a tree and licked its bloody lips.

C)I soon grew fangs; I craved blood and was burned by daylight.

D)Being a vampire is tough work because I have limited working hours.

Holding the torch, you take the quill pen in your free hand, dip it in the inkbottle, and write your answer. You wonder what sort of creature will come out of the coffin this time.

If you write 'A', turn to page 111.
If you write 'B', turn to page 99.
If you write 'C', turn to page 47.
If you write 'D', turn to page 151.

The rocks stop glowing. Everything goes pitch black, including the vid-screen. You know that you have gotten the question wrong, and you feel sorry for D.D. You failed the first challenge given to you.

You take out your computer, and you say, "Carter, on. Turn up your screen brightness all the way." The computer lights up the room.

You explore the room a little more, but there is not much to see. You think about what Mr. Wheatly had said, "It may be that you will have more than one chance to rescue your sister." That's when you resign yourself to going back. You go back the way you had come and manage to scale the rope back out of the cave.

Turn to page 35.

84

"Now, you are trying my patience. You are wrong. You will need to get out of my presence quickly, or you will get yourself eaten."

"Yes ma'am," you stammer and spin quickly away from her. You are too afraid to try the exit that is next to her, so you do the only other thing possible–you run back through the giant chamber. You can sense movement behind you, but you don't turn around to look. The thought of that huge dragon coming after you is too much.

You go towards the narrow passageway, but this time, there is no invisible barrier stopping you. As you go around the last bend into the little chamber, you can hear thunderous snores echoing from down the passage. You know you have escaped the flames of the gigantic mother dragon.

Turn to page 167.

The man behind the desk says, "Bingo! Welcome aboard the executive team, *Quiz Kid.*" He gets up from behind his desk and comes across the room to shake your hand. You feel like you are shaking hands with a frozen piece of crystal out of your mother's china cabinet. He says, "Right thisss way." He is still shaking your hand as he leads you across the room to the far wall. Another panel opens up revealing another hall. He leads you down the hall to another room. As you enter the room, he stays behind in the hall. The panel closes behind you.

The room is like the previous rooms, but the only thing in the room is a chair. You sit down, hoping this will make something happen. As you sit down, a panel opens up, and in walks the crystalline woman wearing a nurse's hat.

"I ssee you are not feeling well today. Been working too hard, have you?" she asks as she walks up to you.

At this point, you don't think it matters much what you say, so you decide to play along. "Well yes," you say, "I have been in meetings all day, and I have a terrible headache. Oh, yes, and I have this strange pain in my diaphragm. My legs are kind of wobbly, and my arm needs to be looked at too."

"I told them disssh wasss going to happen. You need to ressst every once and a while. You just sssimply can't keep going like disssh. Right disssh way, pleassse."

She pulls out a scale from behind a panel and motions you to step on it. You comply.

"Good," she says. "We'll have you fixssed up in no time. Now take disssh tesssst, and anssswer the quessstion." She hands you a piece of paper containing the following statement. "What word is used <u>incorrectly</u> in the following sentences? Select the correct answer. If there are no mistakes, select selection 'D'."

86

A) A dolphin has strength and wit.
B) Your moving higher up the chain
C) moving closer and closer to your goal.
D) [No mistake.]

If you answer 'A', turn to page 111.
If you answer 'B', turn to page 99.
If you answer 'C', turn to page 47.
If you answer 'D', turn to page 151.

"I see," says the dragon. "I see that you are not as smart as you think. You have gotten my question wrong."

For a moment, you look sad, but you can't keep the face for long. You make a fist and answer the dragon. "So, I got one wrong. What about all of the questions I have gotten right?"

"A mere fluke. You're proving your true nature now. You can't expect me to believe that you are smart if you can't get my questions right. Now listen carefully. I have another question for you. Choose the best answer to replace the underlined word or words in the sentence. If the word or words are fine, you may select answer 'D'. Here is the sentence."

Eating you will be more fun than eating a horse.
A) most fun, B) funnest, C) funner, or D) [No change]

If you tell the dragon 'A', turn to page 111.
If you tell the dragon 'B', turn to page 99.
If you tell the dragon 'C', turn to page 47.
If you tell the dragon 'D', turn to page 151.

Chapter Seven
Moving Up In The World

When you land this time, you are more prepared, and you aren't dazed as badly as before. Although the air is clear, the awful goblin stench still clutches to you like a bad memory. You think to yourself, *It's going to take a week of baths to get rid of this disgusting odor.*

You notice that your sword and shield are gone, and you see a small black disk in the middle of the floor. You put it into your computer. "Carter, on," you say. "Read the disk."

"Welcome to Aqua Land, *Quiz Kid*," responds Carter.

As you slowly look around, you find yourself in the middle of a cavernous, square room. The room reminds you of old pictures you have seen of ornate bank lobbies. It is neatly covered with gray and white marbleized tiles, and the walls are pure white and enclosed with sparkling glass.

In the background, you can hear faint "elevator" music. You think the music is very uncool. You've often heard it played in the Mega-Mart store where your mom shops. For an instant, it makes you homesick, but it also strikes a chord. Your mission is to rescue your sister D.D. and return her home safely.

In the room is an antique cherry desk with an old-fashioned desktop computer on it. Behind the computer, there sits a person if, indeed, you can call it a person. The person seems to be the figure of a woman. She is very thin and transparent as if made of fine, glass crystal. She has no smooth curves about her; rather, every aspect of her has sharp angles. She is typing mechanically at the computer and takes no apparent notice of you.

90

The crystalline woman speaks for the first time. "Well, I ssshee we've a candidate." Her voice is like the rushing sound of water from a faucet.

As she stands up from her desk, you have to tilt your head back to look up at her. You think, *She must be seven feet tall! She'd make a great center for my school basketball team.*

She approaches you while you sit in the middle of the floor. The figure of the woman bends down and asks in her mysterious voice, "Isssh there anything we can do for you?"

"My sister D.D., where is she? I'd like to have her back."

"Yesssh. Well, we'll ssshee what we can do. Pleassse, follow me."

She straightens up, goes back to her desk, and starts typing on her computer again. You get up and follow her. You watch as she types, and words fly by on the computer monitor. Soon, she settles on a screen and stops typing.

"You'll have to passs our ssscreen tesssst firsssst," she says. "Here, have a ssssheat." She gets up from her chair and motions for you to sit.

You joke, "Can I have a cup of coffee?"

A questioning look comes on her face, and she says in a stern voice, "New candidatesss don't reccceive coffee."

Her response makes you start to laugh. But then she scowls at you, showing teeth that are sharp as ice picks. This stops your laughing.

You sit down in the chair in front of a computer, which has an old-fashioned keyboard attached. There is a statement on the computer screen that reads, "Read the following and find the word that is used <u>incorrectly</u> in the following sentences. Type the correct answer. If there are no mistakes, type selection 'D'."

A) *Algae floats and is feed on*
B) *by others. You float green*
C) *as others eat you for lunch.*
D) *[No mistakes.]*

If you type 'A', turn to page 111.
If you type 'B', turn to page 99.
If you type 'C', turn to page 47.
If you type 'D', turn to page 151.

92

"This one should be easy pickings," says one of the goblins.

"Yeah, we'll takes it this time," says the other.

They resume their attack on you. You know that you have gotten the question wrong, and you feel sorry for your sister D.D., but you fight on bravely.

Before long, one of the goblins hits you in the head with the hilt of his sword.

You stumble backward into the wall and try to regain your balance. But instead of feeling a wall for support, you fall through the wall.

Turn to page 170.

This time, there is an old-fashioned chalkboard in the room, and a glass crystal figure of a woman is writing on the board. Also in the room are a teacher's desk and a solitary pupil's desk.

She turns and speaks to you in the same mysterious voice, which is like the rushing sound of water from a faucet. "It isssh time for your continuing education ssso that you can perform on the job better. Have a sssheat at that ssstudent'sss dessssk while I write a quessstion for you to ansssswer." She goes to her desk that is piled high with old-fashioned parchments and books and searches for a while. She takes a piece of purple chalk and gives it to you. "You want to move up in the world, don't you?" she asks.

Realizing it won't make a difference what you say, you recite a nursery rhyme, "Jack be nimble, Jack be quick, Jack jumped over the candlestick."

After you say this, the woman says, "Yesssh, let'sss get ssstarted then." Then, she writes the following on the board:

_____. A food chain survives because the environment it lives in enables it to succeed. In a desert biome, plants and animals must be adapted to the arid, hot surroundings in order to live. A marine biome affects its chains because of the special requirements of living in water. In order for producers and consumers to flourish, they must fit with their surroundings.

What is the topic sentence that fits the paragraph above?

A) Different biomes affect the plants and animals that live there.

B) Food chains require plants and animals to survive.

C) Marine biomes are special because water is everywhere.

D) Habitat determines what food chain lives there.

94

You go to the board with your chalk in hand and circle an answer.

If you circle 'A', turn to page 111.
If you circle 'B', turn to page 99.
If you circle 'C', turn to page 47.
If you circle 'D', turn to page 151.

After you go through the doorway, a rock slides back into place behind you. You are in a natural cave passageway. You try to get back into the room from where you had just come, but you can't budge the rock. After a few minutes, the torch you are carrying goes out, leaving you in darkness.

You reach for your computer. "Carter, on," you say. "Turn up the screen brightness all the way." You throw the burnt-out torch to the ground.

You decide to make your way down the passageway. This passage is wet, muddy, and curvy. You have to climb up and down at several points. You are getting covered with mud as is Carter. You hope that you can clean the computer off when you get home.

After quite a while, you climb out of the tunnel into open air. You find yourself in the middle of some green woods. You stride off down a hill through the woods until you come to a pathway. The path goes east and west. Since you rember entering the cave at a fairly high point, you decide to follow the path west, which is in the upward direction.

After about 45 minutes of walking, you reach the spot where the blue light had before been coming out of the ground. This time, there is no blue light, but you recognize the rocks and the surroundings. You walk up to the hole, but there is no rope coming up out of the hole.

Turn to page 35.

96

As you push the buttons, you hear more grinding and clinking sounds off in the distance. You wonder what the strange sounds mean. You think it must be a good sign because you are pretty sure you have gotten the question right.

Turn to page 122.

The dwarf is positioned behind the cart at this point, and he pushes you straight out of the room in the opposite direction from the way that you had come into the room. He sings this song as he pushes the cart.

"Roll along, Roll along,
You have had one more last chance.
Roll along, Roll along,
You can't improve your circumstance."

You fear what this might mean. The cart picks up more speed as it travels downhill, going faster and faster. You wonder where you are going; the passageway is completely dark. Finally, the cart comes to an abrupt stop, and you come flying out, zooming down a slippery slide to end with a thump at the bottom.

After sitting in the dark for a minute and getting your bearings, you reach for your computer. You say, "Carter, on. Turn up the screen brightness all the way."

First, you feel sorry for D.D. because you have failed the test. Then, you try to climb back up the slide, but it is too slippery and muddy. All you manage to do is get dirty.

Soon, you decide to follow the passageway. The passage winds on for a while. There are spots where you have to climb up and spots where you have to climb down. There are times when you have to bend over because of a low ceiling. After a while, the cave empties out into the open air in the woods.

You strike out into the woods. After a few minutes, you come to a path that goes east and west. Since you were pretty high when you entered the cave, you decide to follow the path in the westward direction, which is in the upward direction.

After about 45 minutes of walking, you come to the place where the blue light had before been coming out

98

of the ground. This time, there is no blue light, but you recognize the rocks. You walk up to the hole, but there is no rope coming up out of the hole.

Turn to page 35.

From page 23, turn to 58.
From page 24, turn to 132.
From page 25, turn to 121.
From page 29, turn to 92.
From page 32, turn to 136.
From page 33, turn to 163.
From page 37, turn to 105.
From page 43, turn to 78.
From page 44, turn to 80.
From page 45, turn to 74.
From page 50, turn to 112.
From page 54, turn to 51.
From page 56, turn to 84.
From page 57, turn to 96.
From page 58, turn to 26.
From page 74, turn to 51.
From page 76, turn to 34.
From page 78, turn to 143.
From page 79, turn to 169.
From page 82, turn to 160.
From page 86, turn to 60.
From page 87, turn to 77.
From page 91, turn to 31.
From page 94, turn to 130.
From page 100, turn to 138.
From page 104, turn to 109.
From page 106, turn to 70.

From page 107, turn to 162.
From page 109, turn to 135.
From page 114, turn to 145.
From page 115, turn to 107.
From page 117, turn to 171.
From page 119, turn to 79.
From page 123, turn to 144.
From page 125, turn to 44.
From page 126, turn to 87.
From page 127, turn to 109.
From page 129, turn to 28.
From page 131, turn to 53.
From page 133, turn to 155.
From page 137, turn to 76.
From page 140, turn to 160.
From page 142, turn to 74.
From page 144, turn to 166.
From page 145, turn to 97.
From page 148, turn to 142.
From page 153, turn to 75.
From page 155, turn to 71.
From page 159, turn to 33.
From page 161, turn to 40.
From page 164, turn to 25.
From page 165, turn to 24.
From page 171, turn to 97.

100

"Yesss, I ssshee. Your cassse is worssse than I thought. You will have to ssshee a ssspecialissst."

You know that this is bad news. You must have gotten the question wrong.

The crystalline nurse says, "Right disssh way." She leads you to a panel in the side of the room and down a passage to another room. You go into the room, and the panel slides closed behind you.

The only thing in the room is a chair. As you sit down on it, a panel opens on the far wall, and in walks the glass, crystal figure of a man wearing a white lab coat. In his hand is a clipboard. He walks over to you and stands in front of you.

"I ssshee we have a problem cassse today. We will need to exssamine you very closssely." The lab-coat man hands you the clipboard. It has digi-paper on it with an electric pen stuck under the top. You study it, "What word is used <u>incorrectly</u> in the following sentences? Write the correct answer. If there are no mistakes, write selection 'D'."

A) *Being on top can cause many*
B) *problems. Many sharks are*
C) *tormented by dolphins in the water.*
D) *[No mistake.]*

If you marked 'A', turn to page 111.
If you marked 'B', turn to page 99.
If you marked 'C', turn to page 47.
If you marked 'D', turn to page 151.

They sing out, "You are grand at grammar. This could
be your finest hour." They pick you up and put you in
another cart on the other side of the room. They sing as
they push you along.

"Push the cart,
On the track.
Sing this song,
And don't look back."

Turn to page 113.

102

The goblin says, "Well, it gots it right, the dog. I guess we can't beat it." They abruptly halt their attack upon you and stand with their swords at their sides.

You are greatly relieved when their attack stops. You slide backward still wary of an attack.

As you back away, you hear some grinding and clinking sounds off in the distance.

Turn to page 122.

"Your choice is excellent," he sings out. "You're a good student." He pulls a lever on the floor, switching the tracks. He comes up behind you and gives the cart a shove. As he starts pushing the cart, he starts singing another song.

"Chant this tune,
Down the line.
I will croon,
Down the mine."

Turn to page 133.

104

This time, you are ready for the skeletons. You have the first one burnt before it has a chance to swing its dagger. The second and third prove a little more challenging, but you are able to burn them as well.

You say, "Take that, you gruesome beasts."

As before, a door suddenly opens, revealing another passageway. You follow the passage through the dust and smoke into another room.

This space is a little larger than the room with the skeletons, but it has the same musty smell. As in the previous rooms, there is a table in the middle of the area containing a parchment, a quill pen, and an inkbottle. Against the two sides and on the far wall, three old, wooden coffins stand on their ends. You wonder what is in the coffins, but you turn your attention to the table.

You try to be very quiet in order to not disturb anything in the chamber. You read the instruction on the parchment, "Choose the best answer to fill in the blank in the sentence below."

The enemy, _____ holds the sharpest dagger, cuts the deepest.

A) who, B) whose, C) that, or D) which

Holding the torch, you take the quill pen in your free hand, dip it in the inkbottle, and write your answer.

If you write 'A', turn to page 111.
If you write 'B', turn to page 99.
If you write 'C', turn to page 47.
If you write 'D', turn to page 151.

"Very good," he sings out. He pulls another lever on the floor, turning the track on the ground. He comes behind the cart and pushes you. He starts singing another song as he pushes you down a passage.

"Roll along, Roll along,
Enjoy your ride along.
Roll along, Roll along,
While you sing a song."

You again enjoy your ride as you whiz down another passageway to another room. You don't sing a song like he told you to though.

Turn to page 116.

106

The slab falls back, forming a sort of drawbridge over a deep cavern. You pause before crossing it and gather your courage. Using your computer for light again, you hold your breath and don't look down as you cross the narrow ledge. You dread the thought of falling, but soon you come to the other side. On the other side is a tight passage. Down at the end of the passage sits an opening.

As you walk in, the room is lit by the same glowing blue rock on the ceiling. This room is dryer and cleaner. There is a man sitting in a wooden chair with his back toward you. He rises from his chair and turns toward you. As you look, you see that he has no face. Where his face is supposed to be is covered in a smooth pink skin. The sight of him is frightful, and he makes your skin crawl.

He speaks to you in a deep, husky voice even though he has no mouth. He says, "Welcome, my child. I have a question for you, "Which part of the following sentence is the simple predicate?"

After testing your <u>courage</u>, <u>I</u> must <u>test</u> your <u>wits</u>.
       A   B   C   D

The faceless man gives you the creeps, but you sum up your courage and stay on task, giving the answer some consideration before replying.

If you say 'A', turn to page 111.
If you say 'B', turn to page 99.
If you say 'C', turn to page 47.
If you say 'D', turn to page 151.

You hear a gong sound from somewhere in the room even though there is no apparent source. The two goblins that had been asleep are roused. They pick up some nearby swords and stand before you.

"I don't want any trouble," you say. "I am just looking for my sister."

"Well, you've gots trouble, and plenty of it," says one of the goblins. "You woke us up from our nap, and now you've gots big trouble."

"Trouble is our middle name," says the other goblin with a wicked, snaggle-toothed grin. "Plus, we're hungry, and we needs to eat!"

The first goblin takes a swing at you, moving slowly and awkwardly. Perhaps he is still sleepy. His blow is easy to fend off.

The second goblin also takes a slow swing at you, another equally easy blow to repel.

"Maybe we asks it a question while we're waking up," says the first goblin.

"Yeah, and if it gets it right, we can go back to sleep," says the second goblin with a wide yawn.

They take a step back and drop their swords to their sides. The first goblin asks, "What is 'off with its head' in the following sentence?"

Off with its head, then we can goes to bed.
A) prepositional phrase, B) clause, C) verb, or D) noun

You don't intend on losing your head to any snaggle-toothed monster, so you carefully pick your answer.

If you answer 'A', turn to page 111.
If you answer 'B', turn to page 99.
If you answer 'C', turn to page 47.
If you answer 'D', turn to page 151.

108

He picks up a disk from the arm of his chair and walks over to you. Your hand is shaking a little, but you take the disk from his hand and put it into your computer. It says, "Well done, you have finally arrived. You are indeed a worthy language adversary. If you keep this up, you will soon have your sister back. Welcome to the *Goblins' Lair.*"

The man with no face pulls a wooden lever that is protruding out of the floor. You hear him laugh in his husky voice as the floor gives way below you. You fall down a trap door onto a slide.

Turn to page 129.

You feel there is something wrong with your answer. You aren't sure what it is, but you know there is something wrong.

When you finish writing, the three coffins open, and out stroll three gruesome ghouls. Walking corpses wrapped in tattered rags, animated mummies, move slowly toward you. Their stiff arms are extended straight out in front of them. They make mournful moaning noises. You hold your torch up and swing it from side to side to keep them at bay, but they still come forward. The closer they get, the louder they moan. The louder they moan, the more frightened you get.

On one side of the room, a rock slides away revealing an opening. Thinking you will be able to fight them more easily if they come through the opening one at a time, you go through. But after making your retreat, a rock slides back, sealing the opening.

You examine the room for the first time. You see a table with a parchment, an inkbottle, and a quill pen on it. Besides the table, the room is empty.

This time, you promise yourself that you will do better on your answer. You read the instruction, "Choose the best answer to fill in the blank in the sentence below."

The smoke from the burned undead smelled _____.
A) terrible, B) terribly, C) terribler, or D) terribles

Holding the torch, you take the quill pen in your free hand, dip it in the inkbottle, and write your answer.

If you write 'A', turn to page 111.
If you write 'B', turn to page 99.
If you write 'C', turn to page 47.
If you write 'D', turn to page 151.

110

"Hey, Tan, we has a smart one, we has; better watch out," says the goblin on the left. He raises his sword across his body and crouches down.

"You're right, Pan. I'll watch myself, and I'll bash some brains as well," says Tan, as he too raises his sword.

Tan takes a swing at your head with his sword, but you raise your shield in time to deflect the blow. You counter by swiping up with your own blade, and you can feel that it makes contact with the body of the creature.

You look at your sword, and to your surprise, there is a dark red liquid, almost black in color, dripping from it. The goblin is holding his side, but he has not fallen yet.

This time, it is Pan who swings wildly at your body. Again, you are able to deflect the blow with your shield. You strike again catching him in his face on the cheek. There is more dark red liquid.

You don't wait for them to swing again. You thrust in at Pan, who is holding his cheek, while you duck under another swing from Tan. You catch him full in the belly, and he falls.

Next, you swipe at Tan and catch him with a vicious cut in his chest. He too falls at your feet. You begin to feel nauseous, and you wonder if you have just killed. Is this real or an illusion like the road? You are breathing heavily. Your stomach churns, and sweat comes to your face.

Turn to page 115.

From page 23, turn to 83.
From page 24, turn to 55.
From page 25, turn to 126.
From page 29, turn to 92.
From page 32, turn to 141.
From page 33, turn to 59.
From page 37, turn to 97.
From page 43, turn to 78.
From page 44, turn to 85.
From page 45, turn to 74.
From page 50, turn to 37.
From page 54, turn to 51.
From page 56, turn to 84.
From page 57, turn to 152.
From page 58, turn to 106.
From page 74, turn to 51.
From page 76, turn to 34.
From page 78, turn to 143.
From page 79, turn to 169.
From page 82, turn to 160.
From page 86, turn to 100.
From page 87, turn to 77.
From page 91, turn to 136.
From page 94, turn to 130.
From page 100, turn to 138.
From page 104, turn to 81.
From page 106, turn to 70.
From page 107, turn to 39.
From page 109, turn to 139.
From page 114, turn to 145.
From page 115, turn to 107.
From page 117, turn to 171.
From page 119, turn to 79.
From page 123, turn to 144.
From page 125, turn to 44.
From page 126, turn to 87.
From page 127, turn to 81.
From page 129, turn to 110.
From page 131, turn to 42.
From page 133, turn to 155.
From page 137, turn to 76.
From page 140, turn to 160.
From page 142, turn to 74.
From page 144, turn to 118.
From page 145, turn to 103.
From page 148, turn to 54.
From page 153, turn to 75.
From page 155, turn to 27.
From page 159, turn to 33.
From page 161, turn to 52.
From page 164, turn to 126.
From page 165, turn to 55.
From page 171, turn to 97.

112

"Very good," they sing out. They come toward you and pick you up with amazing strength. They put you in a cart that rolls on the mini-train tracks. They start singing another song as they push you down a passage.

"Roll along, Roll along,
Enjoy your ride along.
Roll along, Roll along,
While you sing a song."

You thoroughly enjoy your ride as you whiz down a passageway to another room. You don't sing a song like they told you to though.

Turn to page 116.

You hum along as you are whizzed again into another room. This time, when the cart stops and dumps you out, you're ready for it, and you manage to stay on your feet.

As you stand up, you notice that the lantern in this room is even bigger than before. You hear two more dwarves—dressed in red suits—singing a song.

"We take our hammer and smash the rocks,
We're glad the grind never mocks.
We never stop; we never rest,
To gather silver for our chest."

They work with hammers and tap a rhythm in tune with the song they sing. They've carved several perfectly formed shapes into the walls. In different walls, you can see a rectangle, a triangle, and a circle. Behind the dwarves stands two pyramid shaped piles. One pile is much like the piles of rocks you have seen before. The other, smaller pile seems to be a pile of silver minerals.

The dwarves put down the hammers that they are holding and dance toward you like the rest of the dwarves have done. They hum, "Da da die and a la la lie. Hello, *Quiz Kid*. Here's a grammar question for you to try." As one, they chant, "Which is the best way of expressing the idea?"

A) Silver spoons and mirrors are objects favored by dwarves.
B) Silver spoons and mirrors are favored objects of dwarves.
C) Dwarves fancy silver spoons and mirrors and objects like them.
D) Dwarves fancy objects like silver spoons and mirrors.

114

"Very talented," you say as you think about the question.

If you tell them 'A', turn to page 111.
If you tell them 'B', turn to page 99.
If you tell them 'C', turn to page 47.
If you tell them 'D', turn to page 151.

You say aloud, "I'm coming D.D. Hang in there." You think, *I just hope I can hang in there.*

After you defeat the goblins in battle, you are able to go down the passageway they had been blocking. As you go down the passageway, it begins to split into two hallways. You decide to follow the one to the right.

You enter a room smaller than the entrance room. The room smells like garbage, and on the floor in the corner are two goblins deeply asleep on a pile of filthy rags. The walls are much the same as you had seen elsewhere in the Goblins' Lair with burning torches hanging up around the room. Nailed onto the farthest wall is an ancient looking parchment with writing on it, which says, "What part of speech is 'you' in the following sentence?"

You will eat dirt and die, human!
A) verb, B) noun, C) adjective, or D) pronoun

Below the parchment are four push buttons affixed to the rock wall clearly marked 'A', 'B', 'C', and 'D'. Ignoring the two sleeping goblins, you reflect on the question for a moment and then make your choice by pushing a button.

If you push 'A', turn to page 111.
If you push 'B', turn to page 99.
If you push 'C', turn to page 47.
If you push 'D', turn to page 151.

116

You whiz into the next room. The cart comes to a halt and dumps you out on your head. As you stand up, you notice that the room has a lantern just as the last one, but the lantern is slightly bigger. More caves are running this way and that way. Again, some have mini-train tracks, and some are without tracks.

The dwarves have carved a V-shape into the wall, and there is again a pyramid of rocks behind them. Other than the pyramid of rocks, you notice there isn't a rock out of place. You can hear two dwarves singing as they work.

"We chip away throughout the day.
We work, work, work to earn our way.
We never stop; we never rest,
To gather tin for our chest."

The singing reminds you of D.D. because she is always singing a song around the house. When the two jolly dwarves have finished their song, they put down their picks and turn toward you. You notice that these dwarves wear blue suits instead of green ones. The blue of their suits matches the blue color in D.D.'s room.

They join arm-in-arm and dance over to you. They hum the same tune with a, "Da da dee and a la la lee. Hello, *Quiz Kid*. Here's a grammar question for thee." As one they chant, "Which is the best way of expressing the idea?"

A) Gathering copper may be grand, but it's not as shiny as bronze.
B) Gathering copper is not as grand as tin and copper together.
C) Copper is grand, but tin and copper combined make shiny bronze.

D) Gathering copper may be grand, but it's not like having tin and copper together, which makes shiny bronze.

You smile and answer their question.

If you tell them 'A', turn to page 111.
If you tell them 'B', turn to page 99.
If you tell them 'C', turn to page 47.
If you tell them 'D', turn to page 151.

118

The goblin says, "Very good, Smarty-Pants. Now, can we get back to some good eats? The chief will be a waiting for you." They turn around and continue with their disease-infested morsels.

You proceed on through the room, trying to not look at their hideous dinner. On the other side of the dining room is a passage leading straight ahead. You go through it, wondering what they mean by "the chief."

At the end of the passage is a room that is slightly larger than the dining room. Here, pillars line each side of the room leading forward and stopping at a throne. Hanging on the two walls beside you, behind the pillars, are spears and shields. The spears are crossed in pairs with a shield hanging over each one. On each shield is painted a crude goblin head surrounded by various bones.

You proceed forward toward the throne. On the throne sits the rather obese king of the goblins. He is asleep with his head craned backward, his mouth open and snoring. On his head there is a jewel-studded crown cocked to the side. On the wall behind the throne there is a tattered tapestry that looks like it was once ornately decorated.

"Well, Chief, where is my sister D.D.?" you say in a loud, demanding voice as you stop before the throne.

"What, what? Uhum! Oh yes, you're here. I've been expecting you, *Quiz Kid*," says the goblin as he stirs himself from his nap. "You have made it through my kinsmen, but you won't get past me! I has got a question for you."

He hands you a dirty piece of old parchment and tells you, "Read this." On the parchment is written, "Read the following paragraph. Choose the sentence that does not belong in the paragraph."

(1) To others, a Goblin is a foul and nasty creature. (2) It sleeps on filthy rag beds and eats the flesh of rotten animals. (3) The Goblin King is the nastiest of them all. (4) A Goblin's smell, though sweet to themselves, makes others want to retch.

A) sentence 1, B) sentence 2, C) sentence 3, or D) sentence 4

You think the goblin king is definitely smarter than the other goblins you have met so far. After taking some time to think, you tell him your answer.

If you answer 'A', turn to page 111.
If you answer 'B', turn to page 99.
If you answer 'C', turn to page 47.
If you answer 'D', turn to page 151.

120

The mother dragon puts her head down and closes her eyes. You know you have gotten the question correct. You go past the dragon to the exit. The passage grows increasingly darker as you go. Soon, the floor gives out below you, and you fall through.

Turn to page 61.

"Guess what? You got it wrong," the dragon gloats. "It is too bad that you have such a forgetful head for grammar," it says sarcastically. "You were so close to succeeding."

"Well, may I have one more chance?" you ask.

"Two questions are all you get. Now it is time for you to go before I turn you into a crispy critter."

At this point, you become terribly afraid and run from the dragon. Not knowing where to go, you try to run back down the passage from where you had come. This time there is no invisible barrier, and you are able to make it back into the passage.

As you turn down a bend in the passage, you feel dragon fire strike your back.

Turn to page 167.

122

This time, you also hear a sliding sound like a rock moving. You think it is coming from the passage where you had just been. You carefully creep back down to investigate. Instead of two passages going to the right and left, there are three passages. One goes straight down the middle of the two. The middle passage reveals a long dark tunnel with a light at the end.

You cautiously proceed down this passage. An awful stench fills your nostrils, and it gets worse as you go along the passage. You have finally gotten used to the repulsive odor of the goblins when, all of a sudden, you are faced with something worse. It is worse than any garbage you've ever taken out to the recyclers.

"Whew," you gasp as the odor almost makes you double over in disgust. "That's rank." You try to hold your nose with your sword hand, but the smell seems to leak through the pores on your nose.

When you reach the end, you discover the source of the horrible odor. There are two long tables running down each side of the room. On the table to the left, there are several large dead lizards with bodies that are shredded and half eaten. On the table to the right, there is the carcass of a horse with its head missing. The carcass looks like it has been thoroughly gnawed. Both the lizards and the horse look rotten.

At the table, munching away at their gross banquet, are two more goblins. They don't seem to notice you at first. Then, one of them turns to face you. He has a bit of flesh dangling loosely from his lips. "Not while I'm a eatin'. This is such a nuisance."

The other goblin turns and says, "You're right. I hates that."

The first goblin spits again, "We has a question for you. If you can answer it, we'll let you go through. We hates dinner interruptions. What part of speech is 'goblin' in the following sentence?"

123

The vultures were eatin' on a dead lizard, but we stole it for our <u>Goblin</u> feast.

A) direct object, B) pronoun, C) adjective, or D) adverb

Wow, now they're stealing food from vultures. What repulsive thing is next? you think. *I better be right on this one, or I might wind up being the goblins' feast.* Contemplating the choices, you prudently answer the question.

If you answer 'A', turn to page 111.
If you answer 'B', turn to page 99.
If you answer 'C', turn to page 47.
If you answer 'D', turn to page 151.

124

You hand the clipboard back to the iceman. "I ssshee we have management material here. Good. Follow me." He leads you to the other side of the room where a panel opens up. You follow him through the doorway and down another hall.

The hall ends where another panel opens up, revealing another room.

At a desk in the room sits a crystal figure of a man. He wears a glass, polka-dot bowtie, and he has his hands up behind his head and his feet up on the desk. You get a closer look at the bowtie, and you see that it has green spots on it. Much to your amazement, the spots look like seaweed.

He speaks in the same mysterious voice as the others, which is like the rushing sound of water from a faucet. "Ssso, you want a promotion, *Quiz Kid*?" He takes his feet off the desk and leans forward, putting his elbows on the desk. He makes a face at you, cocking his head to one side and raising one pointed eyebrow.

You reply with impudence, "No, I'm just trying to find my sister D.D."

"Well," he says getting up and opening a panel, "We'll have to asssk you a quessstion firssst." He takes a cigar from a cabinet behind the panel and walks across the room. "Can I get you anything?" he asks.

You answer, "No, thanks. Like I said, I just want to know where my sister is." The glass, bowtie man smirks.

He sits back down at his desk and lights his cigar. Before long, he has his feet back up on his desk, and he is blowing smoke rings. Finally, he says, "You won't get that promotion without ansssswering my quessstion firssst." He hands you a black marker and a yellow legal pad with the following statement written on it, "What word is used <u>incorrectly</u> in the following sentences? Mark the correct answer. If there are no mistakes, mark selection 'D'."

A) *Up, up the chain you go.*
B) *Algae and shrimp are food for squid.*
C) *Their goes another lunch, yum!*
D) *[No mistake.]*

If you answer 'A', turn to page 111.
If you answer 'B', turn to page 99.
If you answer 'C', turn to page 47.
If you answer 'D', turn to page 151.

"You are correct," says the second dragon. "Now off you go to my brother." He, too, blows out some fire forcing you along.

You come face to face with the third dragon. "I am really getting tired of having fire breathed on me! Just ask me your question, will you?" you shout, having lost your patience somewhere along the trip.

"Well, aren't we a feisty one?" exclaims the dragon. "You would indeed make a good lunch for me. Maybe we can skip the question and have lunch instead."

"No. I don't think so. You had better just ask me the question, please," you say, having calmed down.

"Please? I like that. Very well then, we'll see if your puny little intellect is up to the challenge. Listen carefully while I give you my question. Choose the best answer to replace the underlined word or words in the sentence. If the word or words are fine, you may select answer 'D'. Here is the sentence."

"You have the underlined smallest brain of all the creatures," teased the dragon.
A) most small, B) small, C) smaller, or D) [No change]

If you tell the dragon 'A', turn to page 111.
If you tell the dragon 'B', turn to page 99.
If you tell the dragon 'C', turn to page 47.
If you tell the dragon 'D', turn to page 151.

After you write your answer, the rock that had closed between you and the skeletons slides back open. The three skeletons scramble into the room. There is nowhere to go. You have to fight them.

After several parries and thrusts and much wild swinging, you find your mark on one of the attacking skeletons. You hit its chest with your torch, and it catches on fire, burning bright and quick. Soon after realizing that you can indeed destroy them, you have the other two in ashes upon the ground.

When the third one falls, a sliding rock panel reveals another passageway out of the room. Once more, a thick dust cloud forms. You proceed quickly down the passage through the dust and smoke and into another room.

This space is a little larger than the room with the skeletons, but it has the same musty smell. As in the previous rooms, there is a table with a parchment, a quill pen, and an inkbottle. Against the two side walls and on the far wall, three old, wooden coffins stand on their ends. You wonder what is in the coffins, but you turn your attention to the table.

You read the instruction on the parchment, "Choose the best answer to fill in the <u>blank</u> in the sentence below."

The enemy, _____ holds the sharpest dagger, cuts the deepest.
A) who, B) whose, C) that, or D) which

Holding the torch, you take the quill pen in your free hand, dip it in the inkbottle, and write your answer.

If you write 'A', turn to page 111.
If you write 'B', turn to page 99.
If you write 'C', turn to page 47.
If you write 'D', turn to page 151.

Chapter Six
Thrust And Parry

Down the trap door, you slide into a room neatly carved out of the rock. The room seems about four times the size of your bedroom. Torches hang from dry walls, providing a faint light. You find yourself dazed by the fall but still alive. It takes you a while to realize that you are facing two horrible looking creatures that remind you of goblins. By the faint torchlight, you see a sword and a shield on the floor. Realizing you may need them, you pick them up and are shocked by how strangely light they are. You are on the fencing team at school, so the sword was nothing new to you. You are also taking JoGo Karate, so if it is a fight they want, you are ready to give it to them.

The awful stench of the room makes your stomach churn as the first goblin asks in a horrifying and disgusting voice, "What part of speech is 'neatly' in the following sentence?"

Wan devoured his midnight meal and <u>neatly</u> picked his teeth with a bone.
A) adverb, B) adjective, C) verb, or D) article

Putting the awful goblin smell out of your mind, you listen to the four choices very carefully before responding.

If you respond 'A', turn to page 111.
If you respond 'B', turn to page 99.
If you respond 'C', turn to page 47.
If you respond 'D', turn to page 151.

The crystalline teacher-figure says, "You don't ssseem to have the hang of thisssh yet. You will need to go to another classs." She leads you down a passage and into another room. As before, the panels slide open and closed for her automatically.

Another old-fashioned chalkboard hangs on the wall. As before, a glass crystal figure is writing on the board. She turns and speaks to you as the last figure did, "It isssh time for your continuing education ssso that you can perform on the job better. Have a sssheat at that ssstudent'sss desssk while I write a quessstion for you to anssswer." She goes to her desk that is piled high with old-fashioned parchments and books and takes a piece of purple chalk and gives it to you. "You want to move up in the world, don't you?" she asks.

The last time you recited a nursery rhyme. This time you simply sigh and say, "Yes."

The woman says, "Yesssh, let'sss get ssstarted then."

Then, she writes the following on the board:

_____. Andy Algae floated merrily along soaking up energy from the sun. Sally Shrimp saw her chance for a tasty treat, and algae was her favorite snack. "Yummy," said Squinto Squid hiding in a cloud of ink waiting for a bite of Sally. But Squinto failed to note that Dilly Dolphin had yet to eat her lunch. Dilly swam in circles showing the joy of a full belly.

What is the topic sentence that fits the paragraph above?

A) The moral of the of the story is, "you are what you eat."

B) This adventure tells us about a day in the life of a food chain.

C) This adventure is about how Dilly Dolphin ate her lunch.

D) The moral of the story is, "You can have your squid and eat it too."

If you write 'A', turn to page 111.
If you write 'B', turn to page 99.
If you write 'C', turn to page 47.
If you write 'D', turn to page 151.

132

Smoke comes out of the dragon's nostrils as he says, "Well, you are not very smart, but let's see if you are smart enough to know what to do if I am about to blow fire at you."

You don't need another hint. You do the only thing that seems possible. You run. You run back in the direction from where you had come. This time, there is no barrier stopping you.

As you make your way down the narrow passage, you can feel the heat from the dragon's fire on your back.

Turn to page 167.

You are in a larger room with three singing dwarves—dressed in purple outfits with pointed hats. The room has a positively giant lantern in it. There are no pyramid piles in the room, but there are four wooden chests lined up on the far wall. The walls are covered with shapes and designs.

The dwarves aren't working like the other ones. They are in the middle of the room singing and dancing a jig. They are passing each other a jug as they sing.

"We count the gold; we count the gold;
The precious metal is in our fold.
Work pays off 'cause we don't rest;
Gold, we say, is the best."

When they finish their song, they dance over to you, humming the same tune with a, "Da da doe and a la la loe. Hello, *Quiz Kid*. Here's a grammar question for you to mow." As one they chant, "Which is the best way of combining the <u>two</u> sentences into <u>one</u> sentence?"

We sang all night long.
We sang about gold.
A) We sang about gold and we sang all night long.
B) We sang all night long and we sang about gold.
C) We sang about gold all night long.
D) Gold is what we sang about all night long.

"I'm happy to hear that you have struck gold," you say as you try to remember the sentences they chanted to you.

If you tell them 'A', turn to page 111.
If you tell them 'B', turn to page 99.
If you tell them 'C', turn to page 47.
If you tell them 'D', turn to page 151.

134

"You gots it right, but I'm still going to bash your head," says the one on the left.

"Yeah, me too," says the one on the right.

They come at you again. This time you are ready. You knock the sword out of the hand of the goblin on the right with a move you learned in fencing class. While he is bending down to pick it up, you whack his head leaving him in a pile on the floor.

This gives you a chance to concentrate on the one on the right. He is fighting desperately as your sword dances. He eventually leaves an opening. You stab forward into his gut, and he falls, making a gurgling sound as he crumbles to the floor like a sack of potatoes.

Turn to page 115.

After you write your answer, you have an uneasy feeling that you have done something wrong. This time two rocks slide open at the same time. The first rock that slides open is the one you had just come through. The second rock is one directly opposite that one across the room. The mummies walk into the room with their arms in front of them. Before you know what is happening, they are upon you, pushing and grabbing for you.

You do the best that you can to fend them off, but you are losing ground. You have only one way to go, out the second door. You make your way for the door, keeping the mummies at bay by swinging your torch.

Turn to page 95.

136

The computer screen scrolls up, and the words, "You are correct," appear.

The crystalline woman says, "You're hired, on trial of courssse. Right disssh way, we have an opening that ssshould match your ssskillsss."

She leads you up to one of the walls of the room. A panel in the wall slides open, and she leads you down a hallway. At the end of the hallway, another panel slides open.

"You sssshall be working here." She points with a finger that looks like an icicle.

You step into the room.

As the panel slides closed behind you, you can hear the sounds of construction. You hear hammers banging and saws whining. Before long, the loud sound of a jackhammer rattles your brains.

In the corner of the room, there is a figure of a man who looks like he is made out of ice crystals. The iceman wears a construction hat. The construction hat looks funny on his pointed head. He has a clipboard in his hand, and he yells over the sound of the jackhammer in the same mysterious voice of the crystalline women, "Ah yessss, I ssshee, a new worker. Good, we need one." The jackhammer stops. Lowering his voice, the iceman asks, "What'sss your ssspecialty?"

You walk up to him. "I don't know what my specialty is. I just want my sister back, if you don't mind."

"Don't know your ssspecialty? Then you don't know your place. How will you ever move up in the world? Here, take disssh and ansssswer the quessstion. It will help usss figure out where to sssend you."

The iceman hands you the clipboard. It has digi-paper on it with an electric pen stuck under the top. You study it, "What word is used <u>incorrectly</u> in the following sentence? Write the correct answer. If there are no mistakes, write selection 'D'."

A) You play basketball, and your
B) team needs a center, but a shrimp
C) like you better stick to playing guard.
D) [No mistake.]

If you write down 'A', turn to page 111.
If you write down 'B', turn to page 99.
If you write down 'C', turn to page 47.
If you write down 'D', turn to page 151.

138

After you answer, he says, "Yesssh, I ssshee. We do have a problem here. Your cassse issh worse than I thought. It would ssseem that we need to take desssperate measuresss to correct the problem. Pleassse follow me, would you?"

He leads you to a side panel in the room. The panel opens automatically for him. He leads you down another passage to another room. He stays outside while you go into the room.

Turn to page 72.

When you finish writing the answer, the rock slides away for the second time. The mummies enter. This time there is nowhere to go. You have to fight them. You swing your torch at them. They make the same ghastly moaning sound as before.

Finally, your torch catches one of them on fire. He burns more slowly than the skeletons and makes a lot of thick, black smoke. It continues moving for a little while as it burns. Next, you have the second one burning and then the third. By the time you are finished, you are coughing up a storm from all of the smoke. The smoke gives off an offensive odor as well and makes you want to lose your lunch.

You can hear a faint grinding noise despite your coughing. Then a rock on the far wall slides aside revealing a hidden passageway. You follow it out quickly to escape the smoke.

You go down a much longer passage into another room. This room is as large as the one with the mummies. It has a table with a coffin lying flat on the floor behind it. The coffin is not old like the previous three you had encountered; it is shiny and new. It has ornate gold lettering around the sides of it in a language you can not read.

When you look up, at first glance, the ceiling seems to be alive. Upon closer analysis, you see that the ceiling is covered with bats.

You hate bats. They always give you the creeps. But you bravely go up to the table and read the parchment that is lying upon the table. It contains this instruction, "Choose the sentence that best completes the paragraph below."

"Let me tell you a story," the vampire began. "Long ago, I lived in a country named Transylvania. I was an ordinary human like you, but on one fateful day, I was

changed forever. While I slept at night a huge black bat bit me on the neck. _____. For thousands of years since that terrible night, I have been a vampire, eternally cursed to darkness."

A) My homeland had many mountains, and I loved to explore them.
B) The bat flew to a tree and licked its bloody lips.
C) I soon grew fangs; I craved blood and was burned by daylight.
D) Being a vampire is tough work because I have limited working hours.

Holding the torch, you take the quill pen in your free hand, dip it in the inkbottle, and write your answer. You wonder what sort of creature will come out of the coffin this time.

If you write 'A', turn to page 111.
If you write 'B', turn to page 99.
If you write 'C', turn to page 47.
If you write 'D', turn to page 151.

The computer scrolls up with the words, "That is incorrect." You have it wrong again.

What now? you think.

The crystalline typist comes up to you and says, "I am sssorry; you don't qualify to work in disssh sssection. You will have to follow me to the alternate room. Pleassse come with me." She leads you through a panel in the side wall and down another passage. The passage leads into an empty room. The crystalline typist leaves you by yourself.

Turn to page 72.

142

After you finish writing the letter, you hear clinking noises. The three skeletons come alive! Something is animating them, and they start coming at you. You take your torch in hand and fend them off as best you can.

"Stay back!" you yell. "Get away from me!" You know this can't be real; it reminds you of a horror movie-vid.

After several parries and thrusts and much wild swinging, you find your mark on one of the attacking skeletons. You hit it in the chest with your torch, and it catches on fire, burning bright and quick. Soon after realizing how to destroy them, you have the other two in ashes upon the ground.

You know the skeletons can't be real, but it still makes you feel uneasy to destroy them.

When the third one falls, a sliding rock reveals another passageway out of the room. You proceed down the passage through the dust and smoke and into another room that is similar to the first one.

Three ghastly skeletons stand abreast with daggers in hand, and an old-fashioned parchment sits on the wooden table as before. This time you waste no time; you read and follow the instructions on the parchment right away. "Choose the best answer to fill in the <u>blank</u> in the sentence below."

Only the _____ defeats the undead.
A) swifter, B) more swift, C) most swift, or D) swiftest

Holding the torch, you take the quill pen in your free hand, dip it in the inkbottle, and write your answer.

If you write 'A', turn to page 111.
If you write 'B', turn to page 99.
If you write 'C', turn to page 47.
If you write 'D', turn to page 151.

"Yea! It is dinnertime!" He snaps at your head, and you duck just in time. He swings his tail to try and knock you down, but you tumble backwards out of the way. In fact, you are using the self-defense moves you have learned in JoGo Karate class.

The dragon snarls, showing his razor sharp teeth, and swiftly crawls toward you. Knowing that retreat is the only sensible thing that you can do, you run back the way that you had come. This time there is no invisible barrier to stop you. You run back down the narrow passageway. As you make your way around a bend in the passage, you feel the heat from dragon fire strike your back.

Turn to page 167.

144

"Oh, nuts," says one of the goblins. "Now we gots to interrupt our dinner and fight you."

"Yeah, I hates that," says the other one. "I was really enjoying me dinner."

They each pull out a sword from under the table and stand before you. They still have uneaten shreds of flesh dripping down the front of their gruesome chests as they come at you.

The first one takes a wild swing at you that you are able to avoid easily. The second one just stands there and lets out a loud belch.

The first one takes another swing at you. This time you deflect it with your shield, and you swipe back, missing your mark. The second goblin continues to stand there, staring with a wide-eyed look. As you fight with the first goblin, the second one picks up a leg from the table and begins to munch on it. His mouth is stuffed when he mumbles, "Perhaps we should asks it a question, then we can get back to some eatin'."

"Yeah, maybe you're right," says the other one dropping his guard. You can't resist taking a poke at him after he has attacked you, but he deflects the blow and stands ready. "I'll do the askin' since you're stuffin' your face." He says to you, "What part of speech is the word 'ate' in the following sentence?"

The starving goblin ate nothing but fresh lettuce and celery.
A) verb, B) adverb, C) conjunction, or D) proper noun

If you answer 'A', turn to page 111.
If you answer 'B', turn to page 99.
If you answer 'C', turn to page 47.
If you answer 'D', turn to page 151.

They sing out, "You're a dud; you can't be our bud." They pick you up and put you in a cart on the opposite side of the room. They begin singing.

"Roll, roll, and roll the troll;
Your grammar is very bad.
Roll, roll, and roll the troll;
We find that so very sad."

As you whiz into the next room, you can hear a dwarf—dressed in the same red suit with a pointed hat—singing this song.

"The pick axe is crooked;
You need to concentrate.
The hammer is crooked;
To really get it straight."

The dwarf in the room pulls a lever stopping the cart. You stay in the cart when it comes to a stop. He approaches you and chants, "What is the best way of expressing the idea?"

A) *A silver chalice holds fine mulled wine.*
B) *Wine that is mulled is held in a silver chalice.*
C) *Mulled wine fills a silver chalice that is fine.*
D) *A chalice made of silver holds a fine mulled wine.*

If you tell him 'A', turn to page 111.
If you tell him 'B', turn to page 99.
If you tell him 'C', turn to page 47.
If you tell him 'D', turn to page 151.

Chapter Eight
Chills In The Dark

You find yourself in the middle of a dark, circular room. The room is the diameter of the family-sized swimming pools in your neighborhood. The area is lit with a single torch sitting atop an ornately decorated metal stand in the middle of the room. There is a musty smell in the air. A thick dry layer of dust covers the floor, and cobwebs cling to the ceiling.

You investigate the room more closely. There are no apparent exits. Seeing nothing of interest anywhere, you turn your attention to the torch in the room's center. When you pick up the torch from its base, you hear a grinding sound like rock sliding along rock. A section of the wall skids out and away, and a cloud of dust flies into the air. After a minute, the cloud clears, divulging a passageway.

You follow the passageway into a large, dark, rectangular room. Upon entering, the room gives you an eerie feeling. The room smells like deep forest after a rain. By the torchlight, you can distinguish three skeletons standing abreast against the far wall. Their arms are folded across their chests. Each holds a dagger in their right hand, pointing towards its jaw. In the middle of the room stands a wooden table containing a rolled up parchment, an inkbottle, and an old-fashioned quill pen.

As you stare at the skeletons, their skulls seem to smile back at you. This makes your heart miss a beat and causes you to inhale a deep breath. You turn your attention from the skeletons to the parchment on the table.

You walk up to the table, unroll the parchment, and

read it. Its heading greats you in bold, Old English script letters: "Welcome to the *Hall of the Undead.* Follow the instructions on this parchment explicitly, *Quiz Kid.*" Beneath this is a statement, which reads, "Choose the best answer to fill in the <u>blank</u> in the sentence below."

The flame _____ the skeleton bones.
A) burning, B) was burning, C) were burning, or D) have burning

Holding the torch, you take the quill pen in your free hand, dip it into the inkbottle, and write your answer.

If you write 'A', turn to page 111.
If you write 'B', turn to page 99.
If you write 'C', turn to page 47.
If you write 'D', turn to page 151.

After you write your answer, the coffin slowly opens with a loud creak, and up sits a pale man almost white in appearance. When he opens his mouth to yawn, you see that his mouth has two, long, sharp fangs. "Velcome my fiend. Velcome to my 'umble abode," he says in a Transylvanian accent. His appearance and voice instantly identify him as a vampire, and you stagger back a step.

"You are a verrry adept student of language, *Quiz Kid*. Vould you care for something to eat? Or, drrrink, perrhaps?"

A lingering cough from your bout with the mummies comes out of your mouth as you try to answer, "No. No, thank you."

"Perrhaps, you vouldn't mind it if I had a bite myself," says the vampire as he gets out of his coffin and comes a little closer to you.

Thinking that you may be the main course he has in mind, you respond with an emphatic, "Yes. Yes I would mind. Where are you hiding my sister?"

"All in good tiiime, my dearrr fiend. All in good tiiime."

The man is dressed in black, and he has a cape with red lining. He takes his cape from his back and wraps it around himself. "Vhy don't you drop that nasty torch my fiend?" he hisses.

"I prefer to hold it, thank you very much," you say as you push it toward him.

"I seee," spits the vampire. "Perrrhaps we can share a drrrink." He produces a glass canter with red liquid in it and two glasses. He pours the liquid into the glasses and hands one to you.

You take the glass and smell the liquid as the man takes his and quickly drinks it. The scent of the dark red liquid makes your stomach do a somersault.

"No, thank you. I'd prefer to not drink anything," you say as you throw the glass down to the floor.

150

Before it hits the ground, though, the vampire swoops down and catches the glass, laughing, "Never vaste guud blood my fiend, neverrr." His speed amazes you, and you begin to get a little frightened. You think that you may end up having to fight him, but he seems much too fast.

He seems to sense your fear for he coos, "Do not vorry, my fiend," and he claps twice. A door opens up behind his coffin. "You may prroceed."

You walk past the vampire and through the door. Walking past him gives you the chills, and you keep one wary eye on him. You walk down the passage behind the doorway. It goes into a small room with a small stone table in the middle of it. On the table sits a little black disk. You put the disk into your computer.

"Carter, on. Read the disk."

"Very good. You have made it through the *Hall of the Undead.* Welcome to the *Mining Facilities.*"

The floor opens up, and you slide down again, dropping your torch.

Turn to page 49.

From page 23, turn to 83.
From page 24, turn to 132.
From page 25, turn to 121.
From page 29, turn to 92.
From page 32, turn to 141.
From page 33, turn to 59.
From page 37, turn to 97.
From page 43, turn to 165.
From page 44, turn to 80.
From page 45, turn to 104.
From page 50, turn to 37.
From page 54, turn to 51.
From page 56, turn to 84.
From page 57, turn to 152.
From page 58, turn to 26.
From page 74, turn to 51.
From page 76, turn to 124.
From page 78, turn to 143.
From page 79, turn to 38.
From page 82, turn to 160.
From page 86, turn to 100.
From page 87, turn to 43.
From page 91, turn to 31.
From page 94, turn to 53.
From page 100, turn to 41.
From page 104, turn to 109.
From page 106, turn to 70.

From page 107, turn to 162.
From page 109, turn to 135.
From page 114, turn to 30.
From page 115, turn to 154.
From page 117, turn to 171.
From page 119, turn to 79.
From page 123, turn to 144.
From page 125, turn to 44.
From page 126, turn to 43.
From page 127, turn to 109.
From page 129, turn to 28.
From page 131, turn to 42.
From page 133, turn to 155.
From page 137, turn to 124.
From page 140, turn to 160.
From page 142, turn to 104.
From page 144, turn to 166.
From page 145, turn to 97.
From page 148, turn to 54.
From page 153, turn to 102.
From page 155, turn to 71.
From page 159, turn to 33.
From page 161, turn to 40.
From page 164, turn to 25.
From page 165, turn to 24.
From page 171, turn to 46.

152

You hear a gong sounding from somewhere in the room even though there is no apparent source. The two goblins that had been asleep are roused. They pick up some nearby swords and stand before you.

"Oh no," you stammer. "Look, I don't want to fight you. I'm just looking for my sister."

"Well, you're gonna fight," hollers one of the goblins. "You disturbed us from our sleep, and that's grounds for fightin'. Right Lan?"

"Yeah. You best get ready; we is gonna skin and roast you. Right Wan?" says Lan.

"You bet, people-ka-bob sure sound like a good dinner," snorts Wan.

Lan makes the first move. He thrusts forward with his sword. You knock his blade down with your own sword. Then Wan takes a swing at your head. You can feel the air move in front of your face as he barely misses his mark.

You try to mount an offense, but somehow you can't manage to penetrate their defense. Even in their sleepy state, they seem too adept.

They are fully awake and moving in fast for the kill. Several more swings are taken, and you are barely able to defend yourself.

"I think we could beats it Wan," pants Lan.

"Yeah, we could," says Wan, breathing hard. "But the boss says we gots to ask it a question."

"You're right," says Lan. "I'll ask; I'm smarter than you is."

Then Wan takes another wild swing at you. Barely letting up from their attack, Lan asks, "What part of speech is 'a' in the following sentence?"

What will kill you, a thrust or parry?
A) adverb, B) linking verb, C) verb, or D) article

153

"A thrust!" you shout, jabbing forward with your sword. It is extremely difficult to concentrate while under attack, but you do the best you can.

If you answer 'A', turn to page 111.
If you answer 'B', turn to page 99.
If you answer 'C', turn to page 47.
If you answer 'D', turn to page 151.

154

You hear some grinding and cranking sounds off in the distance, but nothing else seems to happen. The two goblins are not roused, and you see nothing else of interest in the room. You have a pretty good feeling, because you think you have gotten the question right.

Turn to page 57.

They sing out, "How could you get it wrong? You have been so strong!" From this you gather that you have gotten the question wrong. You don't have too much time to think about it, though, as they are singing again.

"You're on the verge of solving our rhyme;
Think harder for your answer this time.
The three of us will give you our test;
We know you'll pass 'cause you are the best."

The three dwarves are still dancing, and the one in the middle is holding the jug. He starts blowing into the jug making a rhythm for another tune. They approach you and chant, "Which is the best way of combining the <u>three</u> sentences into <u>one</u> sentence?"

Bladen Oakhand was a dwarven king.
Bladen Oakhand wore a golden crown.
Bladen Oakhand lived under the mountain.

A) The dwarven king Bladen Oakhand lived under the mountain and wore a golden crown.
B) Bladen Oakhand was a dwarven king who wore a golden crown under the mountain.
C) The dwarven king, Balden Oakhand, wore a golden crown under the mountain.
D) Bladen Oakhand lived under the mountain, was a dwarven king, who wore a golden crown.

If you tell them 'A', turn to page 111.
If you tell them 'B', turn to page 99.
If you tell them 'C', turn to page 47.
If you tell them 'D', turn to page 151.

Chapter Ten
Fiery Trials

You find yourself in a dark chamber. A faint light radiates from a strange, glowing, purple rock formation on the ceiling. The rock resembles a bunch of long, shining worms. The chamber looks like a natural cave with stalactites and stalagmites. You are nearly overcome by a suffocating heat, which doesn't make any sense to you, since you thought most caves were cool.

You put the chip handed to you by the dwarves into your computer. You say, "Carter, on. Read the disk."

"Welcome to the *Dragon's Lair, Quiz Kid,*" Carter responds.

You think, *Well, that explains the heat.*

You see a small narrow passageway leading out of the chamber. You follow it. It winds around a little before dumping you into a gigantic chamber. The chamber is wide enough to hold several houses end to end, and it is longer than it is wide. Giant stalactites and stalagmites are spread throughout the room. Purple glowing rocks that look like somewhat larger worms again provide light. You see several dragons in the room. This frightens you immensely and makes your mind start racing, but you stand firmly on your feet.

There is a huge exit on the other side of the chamber next to one quite large dragon, the biggest of the dragons. This immense beast lies asleep on a pile of gold. You start making your way cautiously across the room toward the exit.

You don't go far when all the smaller dragons come upon you very quickly. They bare their teeth, hiss, swing their long tails, and crouch down, ready to pounce. Not wanting to be a dragon snack, you turn and run away as fast as you can. You reach the passageway where you entered the large chamber and exit running back towards the smaller chamber. You hope that the dragons cannot follow you down its narrow path. This thought proves correct as they stop outside the entrance.

What now? you think. You are trapped in your little stronghold, and there is no way out except through the dragons. You tell yourself that they aren't real, just an illusion, and you have to go out and face them. But this brave self-talk doesn't seem to work. Maybe The Illusionist can make them hurt you. You are just too frightened, so you sit down on a rock and put your head on your hands. You scratch your head and try to come up with an idea of how to get out of this mess.

After spending some time thinking, you decide to go back and sneak a peek out of the passageway. As you cautiously crane your head out of the entrance, you see that the dragons have all moved away and are now somewhat back inside the cave. They are quite still. You decide to try sneaking past them again. Stepping very softly, you hope that they won't hear you. Before you have gotten very far, though, the dragons start charging toward you again.

You turn and run but immediately crash into something hard and solid. You fall abruptly on your back with a thud; an invisible barrier is blocking your exit. The dragons are upon you instantly. One of them pounces, pinning you below his body. He weighs a ton, and it feels like you are going to be crushed to death.

"Now I've got you," it hisses in its snake-like voice. The dragons can talk. This surprises you, but you can't think about it much since you are about to be squished to death.

"Well, Hello," says the dragon on top of you. "You are quite a youngster, I see. Why, I am *much* older and bigger than you are. Lizards keep growing every year they are alive, and I have been alive for a very long time, as have all my brothers."

"Yes, I see. Well, would you please get off of me if you don't mind?" you manage to gasp, even though it is hard to catch your breath.

"Don't mind? Well no, I don't mind, but you must first answer my question if you want me to get up. Listen carefully. Choose the best answer to replace the underlined word or words in the sentence. If the word or words are fine, you may select answer 'D'. Here is the sentence."

The ancient dragon crush the puny human.
A) crushing, B) will crushed, C) crushes, or D) [No change]

You can hardly think with this big dragon sitting on your chest, but you do the best you can.

If you tell the dragon 'A', turn to page 111.
If you tell the dragon 'B', turn to page 99.
If you tell the dragon 'C', turn to page 47.
If you tell the dragon 'D', turn to page 151.

160

You finish writing your answer, but you feel uneasy about your choice. You are pretty sure you have done something wrong. As you finish writing the letter, the coffin opens and up sits a pale man almost white in appearance. When he opens his mouth to yawn, you see that his mouth has fangs. "Velcome. Velcome to my 'umble abode," he says in a Transylvanian accent. His appearance and voice instantly identify him as a vampire, and you stagger back a step.

The vampire turns into a huge bat and begins flapping his wings. You think your eyes are going to be poked out. The bat comes at you. You quickly look around for an escape route. A rock on one of the walls slides open. You rush for the doorway with your arms above your head.

You find yourself in an empty room. You hear a sound behind you and realize that the bat is coming in after you. You turn around to swing your torch at it.

It turns back into a vampire. He is dressed in black pants and a fancy white shirt. The long black cape he wears has a red silk lining. He takes his cape from his back and wraps it around himself. "Vhy don't you drop that nasty torch, my fiend?" he hisses.

"I prefer to hold it, thank you very much," you say as you push it toward him.

"I see," says the vampire. "Perhaps, we shall ask you a question then. Please take this and read it." He hands you a parchment on which there are several large, dark red stain marks. You are afraid to think about how those stains were made. You shiver and concentrate on the parchment. It says, "Choose the sentence that best completes the following paragraph."

"Let me tell you how to tame a specter. When you find a ghost who haunts, you invite it to be your guest. When you promise to let the specter scare and haunt all the

humans it wants, you have it hooked. Then, when you finally have it to your lair, you lock it in a coffin to do your bidding when the time comes. _____.

A) Specters are particularly nasty ghosts who must be tricked to follow you.
B) A specter is white, floats, and devours all it touches.
C) Specters can be your guests only if you treat them kindly.
D) Ghosts, known as specters, can make good pets if you know how to capture them.

If you answer 'A', turn to page 111.
If you answer 'B', turn to page 99.
If you answer 'C', turn to page 47.
If you answer 'D', turn to page 151.

162

"Aw, it gots it wrong," squeals one of the goblins. "Now we have it for dinner."

They are no longer sleepy, and a valiant fight ensues. You do your best to beat them back, but in the end, you lose ground. They force you back out of the room and down the passage from where you had come. Eventually, you are back in the room where you had fallen through the trap door.

You manage to put up a minor stand in this room. You nick one on the arm and the other on the chest, but instead of making them slow down, it just makes them fight harder.

One of the goblins takes a vicious swing at your head. You put your shield up to block the blow, but the weight of the swing causes the shield to come slamming down on your head. This causes you to stumble and wobble backward into the wall. But instead of finding sturdy rock to regain your balance, you go through the wall.

Turn to page 170.

"Very good, but more questions must be answered before you see your sister. Go to the dragon over there," he says, pointing to the dragon closest to you. Then, he lets you go and blows some fire at you to hurry you along. You don't appreciate this, but you are hardly in a position to argue the point.

"Well, hello," says the second dragon as he crawls up in front of you.

You are able to get a closer look at the dragons now. They have hard, greenish, rectangular-shaped scales on their backs, bellies that are reddish in color, and surprisingly nimble-looking claw hands. They have giant bat-like wings with another smaller claw at the top. Large, cat eyes with narrow slits for pupils are closely set on either side of a short, fanged-toothed snout. In the dim light, their eyes have a strange red glow to them.

"A tiny little human, I see. You are such a puny thing, no match for my great strength, I think. I would love to test you in my own way," he says as he comes closer.

He swings his great tail around and knocks you over. You glare at him in anger. "Why don't you just ask me the question that you have?" you say.

"Why? Is it because you know that if the master hadn't given me directions that I would have eaten you by now?"

"Master. Yes, I would like a word or two with the master as you call him. He's a coward hiding behind his creations. Let him come out here and take your place."

"You are no match for the master; you shall never succeed. Listen carefully while I give you my question. Choose the best answer to replace the underlined word or words in the sentence. If the word or words are fine, you may select answer 'D'. Here is the sentence."

164

I have never <u>ate</u> a human before; I wonder what one tastes like.

A) eaten, B) aten, C) eat, or D) [No change]

If you tell the dragon 'A', turn to page 111.
If you tell the dragon 'B', turn to page 99.
If you tell the dragon 'C', turn to page 47.
If you tell the dragon 'D', turn to page 151.

"You are smarter than you look," says the dragon. "You can go on to my brother now." He doesn't blow fire at you, but you run quickly to the next dragon anyway.

"My little snack has arrived," says the next dragon with a toothsome smirk.

"I see you have met all my brothers. It would be a shame for you to die now. We shall see if your midget-sized head has enough brains or not. Listen carefully to my question. Choose the best answer to replace the underlined word or words in the sentence. If the word or words are fine, you may select answer 'D'. Here is the sentence."

The knight was skilled, but my mother ate him yet.
A) anyway, B) whenever, C) later, or D) [No change]

You are tired of all the insults and threats, but at least this is the last of the little dragons.

If you tell the dragon 'A', turn to page 111.
If you tell the dragon 'B', turn to page 99.
If you tell the dragon 'C', turn to page 47.
If you tell the dragon 'D', turn to page 151.

166

"Aw shucks, it gots it wrong," says the goblin holding the leg.

"Yeah, and now we gotta fights it," says the other goblin, taking a swing at you.

For a minute or so you are only fighting the one goblin, but then the other goblin joins in the fray. The two of them are too much for you. They force you back the way you had come.

They fight well together. As one of them swings, the other swings at the same time, forcing you to concentrate on defense only. You don't have a chance to get a swing at either of them.

"Poor D.D.," you think, but you can't think of her for long. You have to concentrate on the fight that is before you.

You give up a lot of ground. You are back in the room where you had fallen through the trap door at the far end of the room. You fight on valiantly, but eventually you get hit in the head with the hilt of a sword. You fall back and try to regain your balance on the wall behind you, but instead of a sturdy wall, you find there is nothing there. You fall through the wall.

Turn to page 170.

You sit down upon a rock, resting your head on your hands. You are despondent after having gotten two questions wrong in a row. After coming so far, you have failed. You long for your sister D.D., but there is nothing you can do. And worse than that, you are stuck yourself. You can't go back and face those terrible lizards again, and there is no way out of the room.

Just about the time you are going to despair, you see something that gives you some hope. There is a small hole in one of the walls. You wonder why you hadn't seen it before. You move closer to examine it. It is small, but if you were to slide down on your belly, you think you can get through. You are scared of being in such a closed in space, but you know that you don't have much choice.

You get out your computer. You say, "Carter, on. Turn up the screen brightness all the way." You hold the computer out in front of you as you slide through the hole. There isn't enough room to turn sideways in the hole so you continue to hold the computer out in front of you as you go through. You hate the idea that you may have to go back, but maybe it won't come to that.

The narrow hole goes on for about twenty feet before it empties out into a much larger passageway. It is much cooler now, and there are no interesting rock formations. The rock is rather plain and smooth. You follow the passage for quite a while, climbing up and down and crawling at times. The passage seems to generally be going in the upward direction, but it is hard to tell.

After what seems to be a long time, you emerge from the cave into the open air. Soon, you are in a thick, wooded area. You strike out into the woods and eventually come to a path. The path goes east and west. Since you remember entering the cave originally from a fairly high point, you decide to follow it in the westward

168

direction, which leads upward.

After about an hour of walking, you come to the spot were the blue light had been coming out of the ground. This time, there is no blue light, but you recognize the rocks. You walk up to the hole, but there is no rope coming up out of the hole.

Turn to page 35.

The king of the goblins laughs again. This time with even more disdain in his voice, he bellows, "No, that wasn't the answer, and now you will pay." He puts his fingers in his mouth and whistles again. The spears came back to life and are jabbing and swinging at you as before. You fight on hard and long, but eventually you can't hold your arms up anymore. You do the only thing that you can do. You flee for your life.

You run all the way back through the goblin dining room until you reach the room where you had fallen through the trap door.

You try to regain your strength, but the spears are on you again. They come flying into the room. You have nowhere to run, so you fight on bravely. Eventually, one of the spears swings down and hits you in the head. You fall back into the wall behind you to catch your balance, but instead you fall through the wall.

Turn to page 170.

170

All of a sudden, all is black. Your head is swimming.

After what is actually a short time, but what seems to be much longer, you remember your computer. You pull it out. "Carter, on," you say. "Turn up the brightness all the way."

Carter complies, and you can make out your surroundings. The sword and shield have disappeared, and you are in a natural cave. It is wet and muddy. You try to figure out which wall you came through, but you can't find any walls that aren't real. The walls all seem sturdy and hard.

Eventually, you turn and start down the passageway.

It makes a steady climb and twists and turns here and there. There are places where you have to climb up, and there are places where you have to stoop down. By the time you see light at the end of a tunnel, both you and Carter are covered in mud. You hope Carter will not be damaged and that you will be able to clean it off later.

You climb out of the tunnel and find yourself at the edge of a path that runs north and south in the woods. You don't know which way to go, but you figure that up is the right direction since you were pretty high when you went into the cave.

After about five minutes of walking, you come to the spot where the blue light had before been coming out of the ground. This time, there is no blue light, but you recognize the rocks. You walk up to the hole and look. There is no rope coming up out of the hole.

Turn to page 35.

They sing out, "You're not grand at grammar. This can't be your finest hour." They pick you up and put you in another cart on the other side of the room. They sing as they push you along.

"Push the cart,
On the track.
Sing this song,
And don't look back."

As you whiz into the next room, you hear a dwarf—dressed in the same blue suit with a pointed hat—singing this song.

"I keep knocking,
Can't you hear the pinging?
I keep knocking,
Your hollow head's a ringing!"

The dwarf in the room pulls a lever, stopping the cart. You stay in the cart when it comes to a stop. He approaches you and chants, "What is the best way of expressing the idea?"

A) *Bronze swords bend and break and look fancy.*
B) *Bronze swords are fancy, bending and breaking.*
C) *A fancy sword that is made of bronze may bend and break.*
D) *A fancy bronze sword may bend and break.*

If you tell him 'A', turn to page 111.
If you tell him 'B', turn to page 99.
If you tell him 'C', turn to page 47.
If you tell him 'D', turn to page 151.

♀ ♀
quizquester.com
Where readers can practice their skills
and
find out more about our books.

Order Form

Web Orders: www.quizquester.com
Postal Orders: QuizQuester Press, LLC
                4311 Sierra Ln,
                Stillwater, OK 74074, USA
Telephone: 410-747-0003

Please send the following books or products:

_____

_____

_____

❏ **Please send FREE information on special offers and products**

Name:_____

Address:_____

City:_____State:_____Zip:_____

Telephone:_____

Email address:_____

Sales Tax: Please add 5% for books shipped to Oklahoma addresses and 5% for books shipped to Maryland addresses.

Shipping:
US: $3 for the first book or product and $1 for each additional product.
International: $8 for the first book or product and $4 for each additional product.
Call for shipping on orders of more than 6 items.

Payment: Check   Credit card:

Visa   MasterCard   American Express   Discover

Card number:_____

Name on card:_____Exp. date:____/____

Q q
quizquester.com
Where readers can practice their skills
and
find out more about our books.

Order Form

Web Orders: www.quizquester.com
Postal Orders: QuizQuester Press, LLC
             4311 Sierra Ln,
             Stillwater, OK 74074, USA
Telephone: 410-747-0003

Please send the following books or products:

_____

_____

_____

☐   **Please send FREE information on special offers and products**

Name:_____

Address:_____

City:_____State:_____Zip:_____

Telephone:_____

Email address:_____

Sales Tax: Please add 5% for books shipped to Oklahoma addresses and 5% for books shipped to Maryland addresses.

Shipping:
US: $3 for the first book or product and $1 for each additional product.
International: $8 for the first book or product and $4 for each additional product.
Call for shipping on orders of more than 6 items.

Payment: Check   Credit card:

Visa   MasterCard   American Express   Discover

Card number:_____

Name on card:_____Exp. date:____/____

Ω Ω

quizquester.com

Where readers can practice their skills **and**
find out more about our books.

Order Form

Web Orders: www.quizquester.com
Postal Orders: QuizQuester Press, LLC
4311 Sierra Ln,
Stillwater, OK 74074, USA
Telephone: 410-747-0003

Please send the following books or products:

_____

_____

_____

☐ **Please send FREE information on special offers and products**

Name:_____

Address:_____

City:_____State:_____Zip:_____

Telephone:_____

Email address:_____

Sales Tax: Please add 5% for books shipped to Oklahoma addresses and 5% for books shipped to Maryland addresses.

Shipping:
US: $3 for the first book or product and $1 for each additional product.
International: $8 for the first book or product and $4 for each additional product.
Call for shipping on orders of more than 6 items.

Payment: Check   Credit card:

ˈsa   MasterCard   American Express   Discover

ˈ number:_____

ˈn card:_____Exp. date:____/____